THE KAT SINCLAIR FILES

BY MICHELLE SCHUSTERMAN

GRAVEYARD SLOT

Grosset & Dunlap
An Imprint of Penguin Random House

THiS ONE'S FOR THE THiNG THAT'S ALWAYS IN THE MiRROR BEHiND YOU—MS

GROSSET & DUNLAP
Penguin Young Readers Group
An Imprint of Penguin Random House LLC

Penguin supports copyright. Copyright fuels creativity, encourages diverse voices, promotes free speech, and creates a vibrant culture. Thank you for buying an authorized edition of this book and for complying with copyright laws by not reproducing, scanning, or distributing any part of it in any form without permission. You are supporting writers and allowing Penguin to continue to publish books for every reader.

Text copyright © 2016 by Michelle Schusterman. Cover illustration copyright © 2016 by Stephanie Olesh. All rights reserved. Published by Grosset & Dunlap, an imprint of Penguin Random House LLC, 345 Hudson Street, New York, New York 10014. GROSSET & DUNLAP is a trademark of Penguin Random House LLC. Printed in the USA.

Book design by Kayla Wasil

Library of Congress Cataloging-in-Publication Data is available.

ISBN 9780448479811

10 9 8 7 6 5 4 3 2 1

CHAPTER ONE
THE BRIDESMAID OF FRANKENSTEIN

Rumorz
All the celebrity gossip you need (and then some)!
What's Next for *P2P*? by Shelly Mathers

Fright TV's *Passport to Paranormal* had a close encounter of the crazy kind last week while shooting an episode in an abandoned Brussels prison. Filming was interrupted when former host Emily Rosinski burst in, attacking her old flame (and the show's psychic medium) Sam Sumners. And if the most obsessive fans are to be believed, the show was dealing with a rather nasty spirit they picked up in Rotterdam. Unfortunately, viewers didn't get to see a lot of the action in last night's episode (although the show enjoyed its highest-ever ratings, thanks to all the buzz). But many fans are getting their behind-the-scenes fix on a blog run by host Jack Sinclair's daughter, Kat. Are her creepy photos and spooky stories fact or fiction? This reporter doesn't care, so long as it's entertaining.

PIRATE ghosts and knife-wielding stalkers are nothing compared to the nightmare that is shopping for bridesmaid dresses. Those things are the worst kind of villain. That empire-waist halter looks so pretty and innocent on the hanger, luring you into a false sense of security—until you're locked in a dressing room together with no escape route. Then it turns on you, strangling your neck with its scratchy lace and digging its beads into your flesh, cinching too tight around your waist but hanging all loose in the chest like it's mocking you. *Hey, I look great on that bridal-magazine model! Maybe I'm not the monster here.*

My mom dragged me to five different dress shops last week. Her soon-to-be-stepdaughter Elena paraded around in poofy flower-girl dresses and screamed like a vampire's victim until the attendants let her try on the sparkly tiaras and necklaces locked up in glass cases, while I fought countless satin monstrosities. And my mom, a professional photographer, documented every grim moment with her camera. *Flash!* A-line Abomination. *Flash!* Evil Empire Waist. *Flash!* The Bustier of Despair. It was *Nightmare on Chiffon Street*, starring Kat Sinclair.

The worst part? I never even agreed to be in the wedding.

When Mom tried to ask if I'd be a bridesmaid over the phone a few weeks before, I changed the subject. She never asked again. Instead, she acted like I agreed to do it. That's how my mom operated: She pretended everyone was totally on board with whatever she did and left it to them to say otherwise. That way she could do whatever she wanted without worrying about other people's feelings, and somehow they were the ones stuck feeling guilty when they finally spoke up.

And I fell for it every time. There I was, boarding a plane to Miami with my dad after two weeks in Chelsea, Ohio, and

I still hadn't told Mom I'd rather be the bride of Frankenstein than a bridesmaid at her wedding.

"Window or aisle?" Dad asked, cramming his massive duffel bag into the overhead bin. I responded by ducking under his arm and flopping down next to the window. Our seats were right over the wing, which made me miss Grandma. (Her favorite episode of *The Twilight Zone* was about a guy who kept seeing a gremlin on the wing of the plane during his flight. We'd binge-watched a few seasons last weekend.)

After tucking my backpack under the seat in front of me, I pulled my iPod out of my pocket and started untangling the headphones. Two-and-a-half-hour flight to Miami; almost eight hours of horror movies to choose from. Of course, after Miami came a nine-hour flight to Brazil. But I figured I'd sleep at least a few hours since it was an overnight flight. Not too much, though—ghost hunters didn't exactly keep normal sleeping schedules.

While the flight attendants went over the usual safety stuff, Dad distractedly scrolled through e-mails on his phone. I wondered how he felt about returning to hosting *Passport to Paranormal*. He really loved the job, but I knew he still felt guilty about what happened back in Brussels. Like it was his fault the show's first host showed up and attacked me.

Terrifying? Yes. But hey, it turned out to be *great* for *P2P*'s ratings.

Dad pocketed his phone as the flight attendant passed

by, checking our seatbelts. When the plane began pulling away from the gate, he turned to me and cleared his throat.

"Kat, there's something we need to talk about."

I groaned. "*Dad.* We did the safety-lecture thing already. No going anywhere by myself. Phone and calling card on me at all times. No more provoking crazy stalkers on the forums—although to be fair, Emily started it—"

"Not about safety," Dad cut in. "About your...involvement with the show."

"You mean my blog?"

My "behind-the-scenes look at the most haunted show on television" had started out as a way for me to keep up with Grandma and my best friends, Trish and Mark. But then some of the *P2P* fans found it. And after the whole Emily debacle, I was up to a few thousand followers. Which was pretty cool, but also kind of intimidating.

"I had a call with Thomas Cooper while you were at your mother's house," Dad said slowly. "Fright TV's noticed how popular your blog is with the show's fans. Especially the, er, younger demographic."

"You mean kids?"

Dad nodded. "Thomas sees this as an opportunity to attract more young viewers to *P2P*. Expand our audience."

"So, what, he wants me to blog more or something?"

"No, he . . ." Dad paused, studying me. "He wants you to be *on* the show."

I stared at him. "Like . . . on TV?"

"Yup. What do you think?"

"I don't want to."

The words spilled out quickly, even though I'd barely had time to process what Dad was saying. But after enduring a full week of dressing-room "fashion shows," just the thought of more on-camera time made me want to crawl into a hole and never come out. And this would be on *television*. If seeing photos of myself on my mom's Facebook page made me cringe, how could I possibly handle seeing myself on TV? *Flash!* Ghastly Girl, Coming Soon to a Screen in Your Living Room.

Dad gave me a funny smile. "I thought you might not be wild about the idea. You don't have to do it," he added quickly. "But Lidia and I promised we'd at least ask you and Oscar."

"They want Oscar on the show, too?"

"Mm-hmm."

Oscar Bettencourt was the producer's nephew. We kind of drove each other crazy at first, but eventually we became friends. I imagined what his expression probably looked like when Lidia asked him to be on *P2P*, and I grinned. Neither of us really liked to admit it, but we were a lot alike. I couldn't imagine he'd want to be on TV, either.

I braced myself against the back of my seat as the plane picked up speed. "Oscar'll say no, too."

"You think so?"

I snorted. "I know so. Tell Mr. Cooper thanks, but no thanks."

It might have been my imagination, but I thought Dad looked a little relieved. Our plane roared into the sky, and ten minutes later I was watching *Jaws* devour its first helpless victim and wondering if shark attacks were common on the beaches in Brazil.

After a surprisingly short wait in the customs line, I tucked my passport back into my bag and followed Dad through the crowded international terminal of the Miami airport. The theme music from *Jaws* was still playing in my head. *Da dum . . . Da dum . . . Da dum, da dum . . . Da-dum-da-dum-da-dum-da-dum—*

"Kat!"

I turned sharply, whacking a bearded guy in the arm with my backpack. "Sorry!" I called after him. A few feet away, Mi Jin Seong dropped her duffel bag, spread her arms wide, and looked at me expectantly.

"Well?" she said, and for a moment I thought she wanted a hug. Then I noticed her shirt and burst out laughing.

"Nothing like seeing my almost naked mother-in-law on a T-shirt," Dad said wryly as we dragged our suitcases over to *Passport to Paranormal*'s intern. After giving Mi Jin a quick hug, I pulled my phone out.

"Can I get a picture for my grandma?"

"Oh my *God*," Mi Jin said, eyes wide. "Seriously, you'd text a photo of me in an Edie Mills shirt *to Edie Mills*? Will she think I'm nuts?"

"Are you kidding? She'll love it." I took a few steps back and centered her in the screen. Mi Jin was a huge fan of Grandma's from back in her horror B-movie star days. The poster from Mi Jin's favorite Edie movie, *Vampires of New Jersey*, was featured on the front of her T-shirt: a younger version of my grandmother with ridiculously teased-up black hair, deathly pale skin, and an embarrassingly skimpy bikini, standing on a boardwalk with her spike-heeled foot on the chest of a dead surfer. Blood trickled from her mouth, and you could see two tiny holes in the guy's neck. The tagline at the bottom said: *This Summer, the Shore Is Really Going to Suck.*

Mi Jin struck a pose just like on the poster, putting her foot on her duffel bag and puckering her lips. I snickered as I texted the photo to Grandma.

KS: told u Mi Jin loves Maribel Mauls!

Dad shook his head, amused. Then he glanced over my shoulder and his face lit up. "There's Jess!" He hurried over to our gate while I trailed behind with Mi Jin, watching my phone. When Grandma responded, Mi Jin let out a little shriek and flapped her hands.

EM: aw, what a doll! nice to know she appreciates my vampire vixen. unlike some people.

7

"That woman is my *hero*," Mi Jin said fervently as she watched me text. "I rewatched all seventeen of her movies last week. Man, I forgot how great *Return to the Asylum* is. And *The Coven's Curse*, oh my God, remember that scene with the voodoo doll? I can't even—hey, there's Lidia! She looks *so* much better."

Before I could respond, Mi Jin ran off to hug Lidia Bettencourt. I was relieved to see that *P2P*'s producer looked much healthier than last time I'd seen her. Being possessed by a nasty pirate really takes it out of you.

I stepped back, pulled my Elapse E-250 camera from my bag, and flipped it on. A few photos of this *P2P* airport reunion would be nice for my next blog post. I got a great shot of Jess tackle-hugging Dad, as well as Lidia and Sam Sumners laughing at Mi Jin's shirt. Being on this side of the camera was so much more fun. When I zoomed in on Roland Yeske, he stuck his tongue out just as I pressed the shutter-release button.

"Uh-oh, did you run out of purple suckers?" I teased as he walked over, flipping the camera around so he could see his own bright red tongue in the viewfinder. Roland let out an exaggerated sigh.

"Had to wake up so early to make my first flight, I forgot to bring them," he told me, pulling a red sucker from his pocket and peeling off the wrapper. "And that shop over there only had strawberry. Give me grape, or give me death." He popped the sucker into his mouth and shuddered. "Disgusting."

"But still better than cigarettes," I pointed out. Roland's sucker obsession had started after he quit smoking. "Hey, where's Oscar?"

"Went to get snacks for the flight." Roland sank into a chair and glowered up at me. "So. Looks like we're going all Nickelodeon after all."

"Huh?"

"He's talking about you and Oscar being on the show." Sam settled into the seat next to Roland. "Hello, Kat," he added with a smile.

"Hi, Sam," I said. "I'm not going to be on the show."

Roland's eyebrow shot up. "No?"

"No way," I said forcefully. "I don't want to be on TV."

"Sweet." Roland crunched his sucker. "That means Oscar can't do it—the network wants you both together. And no offense, but I wasn't thrilled with the idea of this turning into a kids' show. Neither was Jess."

"Adding a few children to the cast wouldn't necessarily make it a 'kids' show,'" Sam said patiently. "Personally, Kat,

I was hoping you would accept."

"You were?" I said in surprise, and he nodded.

"Spirits are often more inclined to communicate with children. Particularly if they're children as well."

I knew he was thinking of Levi, Lidia's twin brother, who had died when they were teenagers. His ghost had spent weeks trying to send me messages that Lidia was in danger when Dad and I first joined the show.

"They can still communicate with her all they want," Roland said, stretching his arms and yawning. "Just not on camera. Which is for the best—no one'll ever take what we do seriously if we let Fright TV turn this show into some sort of *Haunted Hannah Montana*. Again, no offense."

He gave me a pink-toothed grin, and I crossed my arms. "First of all, saying 'no offense' doesn't magically make what you said not offensive. And second, you're a parapsychologist. Most people already don't take what you do seriously."

"Ouch." Roland clutched his chest, his expression wounded. "Right in the heart, Kat. This is my life's work you're talking about."

I laughed, although I wasn't entirely sure he was being sarcastic. That was the thing with Roland. He was constantly mocking everyone, including himself. He talked about ghosts like they were a joke, even though he believed they were real. Parapsychology might have been Roland's life's work, but sometimes it seemed like no one took it less seriously than he did.

"Hey, Doctor Pain."

I turned to find Oscar behind me holding a plastic bag stuffed with chips and candy bars. "Hey! How was . . . um, how was your trip?" I stopped myself just in time from mentioning Oscar's father in front of Roland and Sam. Lidia might have told them about her brother being in prison for embezzlement, but I didn't know for sure.

Oscar shrugged. "Fine. Yours?"

"Fine."

"Cool."

There was a pause, and Roland turned to Sam. "What sparkling conversation. Maybe we should put them on camera after all."

I rolled my eyes, but Oscar looked confused. "Wait, what? Aunt Lidia said we definitely *were* going to be on the show."

"You were," Roland agreed. "But it looks like it's not going to happen."

"Why not?"

Roland pointed his sucker at me. "Kat doesn't want to."

Oscar's eyes widened as he faced me. "You *don't*?"

"You *do*?" I said in disbelief.

"Uh, *yeah*?" Oscar squinted at me like I'd sprouted fangs. "We'd be on TV, Kat. On *television*."

"Exactly! Why would I want that?"

"Why *wouldn't* you?"

Flash! Tutu'd Troll. My stomach churned at the memory of that particular dress. Elena had fallen over in hysterics when I'd walked out of the dressing room, but my mom still took a photo.

"Ladies and gentlemen, we will begin boarding Flight 2278 to Salvador, Brazil, in just a moment. Please have your ticket and ID ready."

Relieved at the interruption, I knelt down and unzipped the front pocket of my bag to find my ticket. I could feel Oscar still staring at me as everyone around us began to move closer to the gate. As soon as I straightened up, he started in again.

"Why don't you want to do this?" he asked, following me over to where Jess and Dad had claimed a spot in the line. "How many people get a chance to be on TV, Kat? And did you see that article on *Rumorz*? Everyone already knows about your blog, the fans would probably love it if—"

"Having a blog is different than being on a television show," I interrupted. "I don't want to do it, okay?"

Oscar opened his mouth to argue some more, but Jess beat him to it. "Kat, what if we did a trial to see how you two are on camera? I was thinking we could shoot a mini episode, maybe five or ten minutes, of just you and Oscar, and post it on your blog. It'd be a nice way to test this out with viewers before we actually add you both to the cast."

I could feel my face growing warm. "I thought you didn't want a 'kids' show'? That's what Roland said."

"I didn't," Jess said bluntly. "But Lidia and I had a call with Thomas this morning, and the network is dead set on doing

12

this. With *both* of you." I must have looked as horrified as I felt, because her expression softened. "I honestly do think you two might be pretty great," she added. "Thomas made it clear that they aren't going to start marketing the show to younger viewers, which was my concern. They're just hoping to expand our audience by getting kids interested, too. It's not a bad idea."

"No one's forcing you, Kat," Dad added quickly, and I snorted.

"Really? Because it sure feels like I don't have a choice."

"You do," Jess assured me. "Let's just take this one step at a time, okay? Lidia did a little scouting and found a cemetery not too far from our hotel. We have a few days before our first real investigation—how about I take the two of you to the cemetery to shoot a short video for your blog? No TV, no pressure. Okay?"

Not okay. But I couldn't say that, because it really was a pretty reasonable request, and I was too embarrassed to admit that even the thought of posting a video of myself online made me queasy. Especially because I wasn't sure why it bothered me so much. I mean, it wasn't like I'd be wearing one of those stupid bridesmaid dresses on camera. I'd be dressed like me, and no matter how much my mom sighed at my clothes and fretted over my hair, I liked how I looked just fine. So I just shrugged and said, "Yeah, okay."

Dad studied me. "Are you sure?"

"Yeah."

"Awesome." Oscar grinned at me, and I tried to smile back. I was relieved when the line finally started to move. As we shuffled forward, I wondered if Oscar was right. Maybe I *should* be more excited about this. Trish and Mark would freak out if I told them I was going to be on TV. Besides, my grandmother had starred in horror movies. My father hosted a ghost-hunting show. This was in my blood.

That's what I kept telling myself, anyway.

I crammed my bag into the overhead compartment and found my seat: 27F, next to the window. Glancing around the cabin, I noticed we were all scattered. Dad waved at me from a few rows ahead. Roland and Jess were near the front, while Lidia, Sam, and Mi Jin were several rows back. I saw Oscar kneeling on his seat, watching my row intently. When a guy in a Nirvana shirt started to shove his backpack into the bin over my head, Oscar made his way toward us, squeezing around a woman trying to fit a cat crate under her seat.

"Are you in 27E?" Oscar asked, and the Nirvana guy blinked at him.

"Yeah . . ."

"Would you switch with me so I can sit next to my friend?" Oscar pointed back at his row. "30D. Aisle seat."

The guy shrugged. "Sure, whatever."

Oscar slid into the seat next to me, holding out the plastic bag stuffed with snacks. I took a bag of M&Ms and ripped it open. "Thanks."

"Sure." He helped himself to a few, eyeing me. "Sorry you got stuck doing this mini-episode thing."

I smirked. "No, you're not. If I don't do it, you can't, either."

"True," Oscar admitted. "But I really thought you'd *want* to be on the show."

"And I really thought you wouldn't." I popped a handful M&Ms in my mouth. "So . . . how'd things go with your dad?"

Oscar's expression tightened. "All right, I guess," he said, tearing open a bag of pretzels. "I did it. I mean, I told him about . . . you know."

I nodded. Last year, Oscar had gotten expelled for getting in a fight with his best friend, Mark. But he'd never told his dad the reason he'd gotten in the fight in the first place. Oscar had a crush on Mark and told him so. And he'd ended up being bullied—not just by Mark, but by a bunch of other kids, too.

It was something I'd thought about a lot over the last two weeks, when I was hanging out with my own best friends back in Ohio. Every time I tried to imagine one of them turning on me for confiding something that personal, I felt sick and sad.

"What did your dad say?" I asked.

"Not much. I don't know. Actually, he . . ." Pausing, Oscar stared down at his pretzels. Then he shook his head. "Whatever. The point is, I got it over with. How'd things go with your mom?"

"Oh, fantastic," I said in a falsely bright voice. "I got to try on bridesmaid dresses with her and her fiancé's five-year-old daughter. Who, by the way, can scream even louder than Mi Jin."

Oscar looked up. "Aw, I'm sorry I missed that."

"What, a screaming kindergartner?"

"No, you wearing a dress," he said, grinning. "Was it pink? Please tell me it was pink."

"Nope. She picked purple and green for the wedding theme," I told him. "No, sorry—'lavender and mint.' Every dress I tried on made me look like an Easter egg."

Oscar laughed. "I'm sure it wasn't that bad."

"Trust me, it was worse." I glanced out the window as our plane slowly backed away from the gate. My reflection stared at me, and I touched the back of my head self-consciously. To the surprise of no one, my mother had not been pleased to see my new haircut. Especially when she found out I'd chopped off my braid myself. Now my hair was barely long enough to pull into a ponytail, which was how I'd been wearing it. Mom had tried to take me to her salon to "at least get something a little more stylish." But I preferred it exactly like this: short and simple.

It was an argument we'd been having ever since I could remember. She'd make some attempt to, in her words, "girlify" me. I'd hate it. She'd say she was only trying to help. I'd feel guilty. Repeat, repeat, repeat. I'd grown up with a really clear mental image of the girl my mother wanted me to be. Eventually it had turned into a thing—*the* Thing—that I kind of obsessed over. I was doing my best to leave the Thing behind for real this time. But after six months of pretty much not speaking to my mom at all, spending last week letting her force me into dress after dress had been kind of intense.

"Guess I'll have to wait for the wedding photos," Oscar said. "When is it, anyway?"

"April." *But I probably won't be in the photos.* I crammed the last few M&Ms in my mouth and crumpled the bag. Telling my mom I didn't want to go to her wedding would be a lot easier over the phone. It'd probably be best to get it over with as soon as we got to Salvador, if I was going to do it at all.

I leaned back as the plane accelerated, still staring out the window. I was sitting further back than I had on the last flight, but I could see the tip of the wing. When I squinted, it was easy to imagine a gremlin dancing on the other side of my reflection.

From: trishhhhbequiet@mymail.net
To: acciopancakes@mymail.net
Subject: snow day!!

woke up to a blizzard and NO SCHOOL!!!! jealous? oh wait no, you're on a beach. in BRAZIL. :P mark's coming over later. want to video chat??
<3 trish

SCHOOL is so much more bearable in a hammock," Oscar said. I nodded in agreement, stretching my legs and wiggling my bare feet. Mi Jin squeezed more sunscreen on her arms and legs, then tossed the bottle next to her flip-flops.

"All right, I think I see another guy selling ice pops heading this way," she said, pointing down the beach before rubbing the lotion into her arms. "Two more questions on this history worksheet. Get them both right and dessert's on me."

The three of us were crammed side by side onto one hammock like it was a porch swing, our bags and sandals discarded on the white sand underneath us. The bluest water I'd ever seen in my life stretched out endlessly in front of me, making it kind of hard to focus on the Industrial

Revolution. Not that I was complaining. This was pretty much the best classroom ever.

Clearing her throat, Mi Jin peered down at the worksheet on her lap. "In what year was the first telegraph cable laid across the Atlantic?"

"1858," I said immediately.

"Yup. Last one . . ." Mi Jin flipped the worksheet over. "Tell me three ways the Factory Acts affected child labor practices in the UK."

"Made it illegal for kids to work in factories," said Oscar quickly.

"But only if they were under nine years old," I added. "And they couldn't force them to work at night anymore. And . . . um . . ."

"One more." Mi Jin pulled a few coins out of her pocket, looking pointedly over at the ice pops cart.

"And being a kid in the eighteen hundreds really sucked," Oscar announced. "Bye!" He lunged off the hammock, but Mi Jin grabbed the back of his T-shirt. I giggled as Oscar half-heartedly tried to escape her grip, rocking our hammock back and forth.

"No working at night and . . . ," I repeated. "Oh! All working children had to have two hours of school a day!"

Mi Jin let go of Oscar's shirt and slapped the coins into my hand. "Coconut for me, please."

"Got it!" I sprinted after Oscar, who was already halfway across the beach. He beat me to the ice pops cart by half a second. The vendor laughed when I pushed Oscar out of the way so I could get a better look at the options.

"*Qual sabores?*" Oscar asked, and the vendor pointed to each row of brightly colored ice pops as he recited the flavors:

"*Morango, coco, maracujá, manga, tamarindo, e acaí.*"

"*Acaí,*" I said immediately. I didn't know exactly what acaí was—some sort of berry, according to Oscar—but I'd had an acaí ice pop when we got to the beach this morning and it was delicious. Like a mix of raspberry and really dark chocolate.

"*Un coco e un maracujá, por favor,*" Oscar added.

Oscar had told me his Portuguese wasn't great, but I'd heard him use it several times since we arrived last night and it sounded pretty good to me. We watched as the guy pulled three ice pops from the cart: one white, one dark purple, and one bright yellow-orange with specks of black. I took the purple one eagerly, and he handed Oscar the other two.

"*Obrigado,*" Oscar said as I dropped the coins into the vendor's palm.

"*De nada.*"

"*Obrigado,*" I repeated, doing my best to say it the way Oscar had. But for some reason, the ice pop guy laughed.

"*De nada, amiga.*"

We headed back to Mi Jin, ice pops already dripping on our fingers under the midday sun. I waited until the vendor was out of earshot before turning to Oscar. "All right, what was he laughing at? Did I say *thanks* wrong?"

Oscar snickered. "Sort of. You're supposed to say *obriga*-da."

"That's not how you said it."

"Boys say *obrigado*, girls say *obrigada*."

I stared at him. "Are you messing with me?"

"No." He laughed when I elbowed him. "Seriously, I'm not!"

"That's not how it is in Spanish," I said. "Everyone just says *gracias*."

Oscar shrugged. "Yeah, well. Portuguese isn't Spanish. Hey, come this way."

I followed him as he veered off toward the water, cutting a wide circle around our hammock, where Mi Jin was reading a book. She didn't notice when we crept up behind her. But she definitely noticed when Oscar touched her ice pop to the back of her neck. Her scream was so loud, even the vendor way down the beach looked over at us.

"Evil children!" Mi Jin snatched her ice pop from Oscar, laughing. She never seemed to mind his pranks. I kicked off my sandals and flopped down next to her, and Oscar did the same on her other side. The hammock swung lazily back and forth.

"So let's talk about this cemetery trip tonight," Mi Jin said. "Any ideas on what you guys actually want to do?"

"What do you mean?" Oscar asked.

"Well, this is supposed to be like a trial to see how you'd

be on the show," Mi Jin replied, and my stomach flipped over. I ignored it and bit off a large chunk of my ice pop. "And everyone kind of has a role, you know? Jack's the journalist. Sam does the contacting. Roland cracks jokes and occasionally offers actual psychological insight. So what can you two bring? Besides pranks," she added, gently kicking Oscar's leg.

His eyes brightened. "Wait, why not pranks?" he asked eagerly. "The fans leave lots of comments when Kat posts about them. Like that time I locked you in the prison van."

Mi Jin smiled. "Yeah, but we have to be careful with playing pranks on camera. Everyone knows about the trick light bulbs they used in the first episode, thanks to Emily. Viewers don't want to be tricked. Fright TV wasn't thrilled about it, either."

"Aw."

"What do you think, Kat?" Mi Jin asked, turning to me. "Any ideas for tonight?"

"How about not going?" I said dryly.

She laughed. "Come on, I bet you'll have fun. I honestly think you two would be great together. On the show, I mean," she added teasingly. I wondered if Oscar was rolling his eyes, too.

"Why, though?" I couldn't help but ask. "We might be really awkward on camera."

"Speak for yourself, Doctor Pain," Oscar said. "I've seen myself on video, and I found myself quite charming."

"Mmm. The question is, will the viewers will love you as much as you do?"

Mi Jin was still giggling. "See, this is exactly why it's going to work. It's the same reason the fans love watching Roland and Sam. You two have chemistry."

"Ew," Oscar and I said at the same time. Mi Jin sat up, waving her ice pop like a wand.

"Wait, I know—my Ouija board! You guys could bring it to the cemetery tonight. Try to make contact near one of the graves or something."

"That's a pretty good idea," I admitted. We'd had success contacting ghosts with Mi Jin's homemade electronic Ouija board before. Although that was mostly thanks to Jamie and Hailey, Thomas Cooper's kids. Jamie especially had a knack for contacting ghosts. He also had a knack for being extremely adorable.

"But what if nothing happens?" Oscar was saying. "A video of us just sitting around a Ouija board isn't going to be very entertaining."

I hopped off the hammock and slid my sandals back on. "Then we have to make it entertaining," I said. "But without tricks."

"Where are you going?" Mi Jin asked as I picked up my bag.

"Back to the hotel. I have to e-mail someone."

KAT! I can't believe you and Oscar get to be on P2P. Hailey's so jealous. I might be a little jealous, too. :)

About your Ouija question—the more you know about the ghost you're trying to contact, the better your chances. So if you guys go to this cemetery and just pick a random grave, it probably won't work. Remember when we contacted Sonia? We knew a lot about her, how she rescued her brother from Crimptown, and how Red Leer killed her. We even knew what she looked like. Is there any way you could find out more about the people buried at the cemetery? I think that would help a lot.

One more week until winter break! I can't wait to get to Buenos Aires. Hope you guys are enjoying the beach while Hailey and me are freezing to death here in New York. See you soon!

Jamie

Cemitério do Céu Infinito wasn't one of those creepy old graveyards with ancient, cracked tombstones and overgrown weeds hiding the names of the deceased. Instead, it was a sea of beautiful white statues, ornate tombs, and stucco arches that Dad called "perfect examples of late Baroque architecture." He was up ahead with Jess and Mi Jin, who were both getting footage of the cemetery.

Oscar and I trailed behind. "Still nervous?" he asked me.

I didn't answer. My plan for getting over my anxiety was to just not think about it until it was happening. Shyness had never been my thing. I reminded myself that this was not the same as my mom's Maid of Horror slideshow.

"Do you have that picture?" I asked instead. Oscar held

it up in response. It was a photo we'd printed of a tabloid magazine cover. A glamorous woman with thick, wavy black hair had her arm around a skinny girl in a hospital gown. Both were beaming, even though the girl was clearly sick. The headline read *Tragédia Segredo de Flavia*.

"All right, kids!" Jess called, camera hanging at her side. "I think we found it."

She gestured to one of the larger headstones, and Oscar and I hurried over. He shined his flashlight so we could read the name: *Flavia Arias*. Several dozen bouquets of flowers were piled on the tomb and the ground. A few feet away, several more bouquets lay in front of a smaller tombstone. I moved closer to read the inscription just as Jess cleared her throat.

"So here's what I'm thinking," she said, and I looked up. "First I want to start with Kat talking about why she chose this particular grave, then we'll set up the Ouija board." Handing her camera to Mi Jin, Jess took my arm and positioned me next to the larger headstone. "Mi Jin and I are going to film from different angles," she told me. "But I want you to face your dad, okay? You're not talking to the camera or viewers or anything like that. You're just telling your dad what you know about this person like we're not even here. Very casual, very relaxed. Sound good?"

I nodded, taking the picture from Oscar. He moved next to Mi Jin, while Dad took several steps back from the tomb and faced me. He smiled, and I tried to smile back and ignore

Jess and Mi Jin and their cameras.

"Whenever you're ready," said Jess, and I took a deep breath.

"This is the grave of Flavia Arias, a singer who was born in Salvador," I began, hating the way my voice shook just a little. "She had a bunch of hit songs back in the '90s and was starting to get famous internationally. Then one day she just stopped performing: no more tours or albums, nothing."

Dad nodded encouragingly, and I stood up a little straighter.

"Last year, she died in a car accident," I told him. "And it wasn't until her funeral that everyone found out the truth about why she gave up her singing career." I held up the picture, and Mi Jin stepped closer with her camera. "Her daughter, Ana, had cancer. Flavia wasn't married, and Ana was her only child. She was really protective of her—she didn't want Ana to have to deal with the media, especially after she got sick. So when she heard Ana's diagnosis, she quit singing and stopped appearing in public. She kept Ana's treatments really private, too. When Ana died in 1998, Flavia managed to keep it out of the news. She kind of turned into a recluse afterward, and eventually, the media lost interest in her. But when Flavia was killed in that car accident last year, everyone found out about Ana. Because Flavia had bought this plot years ago so she could be buried next to her daughter."

I pointed to the smaller tombstone. "That's actually who Oscar and I are going to try to contact. Ana Arias."

Jess lowered her camera, and I exhaled shakily.

"Kat, that was *awesome*," said Mi Jin. To my surprise, Jess nodded in agreement.

"I mean . . ." She glanced over at Dad, who was beaming proudly at me. "How in the world did you learn all that stuff about her daughter?"

"I looked online to see if any famous people were buried here," I told her. "Everything I found was in Portuguese, but Oscar translated most of it. There are a few other celebrities and politicians, but when I read about Flavia's daughter, I figured she'd be the best one to try to contact. She was eleven when she died, and Sam always says the ghosts of children are more likely to contact other children, and . . . Why are you both looking at me like that?" I demanded, because now Jess wore Dad's same goofy smile.

"Future journalist," Dad said triumphantly, raising his arms over his head. I wrinkled my nose.

"What?"

"You treated this like an assignment," Jess told me, pointing to the picture in my hand. "All I said was, 'Hey, let's go film something in this cemetery.' And you did the research. You found the story. Like father, like daughter."

I rolled my eyes. "If you say so. Ouija time?"

"You bet." Jess snapped back into director mode. "Oscar, Kat, over here. I want to get you two on either side of the board so we can see the tombstone between you. Mi Jin, this way . . ."

I sat cross-legged opposite Oscar, carefully moving a few bouquets out of the way. Future journalist? I wasn't so sure about that. Although I actually had enjoyed researching Ana. In fact I'd gotten so caught up in it, I'd accidentally blown off video chatting with Trish and Mark.

Oscar unfolded Mi Jin's electronic Ouija board and flipped the switch on the circuit board that was set between *YES* and *NO*. I jiggled the planchette, which held the mouse, over the letters until its little red light started winking.

"Remember, no faking it," I told Oscar in a low voice. "If this doesn't work, we'll just have to figure something else out. We can't trick the viewers."

"Yeah." He drummed his fingers on his knee, eyeing Jess. "Although you know if we do somehow contact Ana, viewers will think it's fake, anyway."

"Not all of them," I pointed out. "Some of the fans really believe in this stuff."

"Right. So . . ." Oscar leaned closer, tapping the planchette. "What difference would it make if we moved this thing around instead of a ghost?"

"Oscar . . ."

"It's like you said," he whispered. "No matter what, some people will believe and some will think we're faking it. But that's better than nothing happening at all, right? We need to make it entertaining. That's what Roland always says."

I opened my mouth to protest, but Jess suddenly crouched in front of us, setting her camera on a short, squat tripod. Mi

Jin stood behind the tomb, getting an overhead shot of us with the Ouija board.

"Okay," Jess said. "I'm not here, Mi Jin's not here, don't worry about looking into the cameras. Just talk to each other about Flavia and Ana, then give the board a try. And remember, we're going to edit this, so don't worry about whether things feel slow or boring."

I gave Oscar a pointed look, and he made a face.

"Ready?" asked Jess.

I nodded, wiping my palms on my shorts. Oscar bounced up and down a little. I wondered if he was nervous, too. The thought made me feel slightly better.

"All right, here we go." The red light on Jess's camera blinked on again.

Immediately, Oscar picked up the picture of Flavia and Ana and made a show of leaning it against Ana's tombstone. "*Tragédia Segredo de Flavia,*" he said in a loud, solemn voice, pointing to the headline. "All the stories we found online focused on Flavia Arias. But this story is really more about Ana. Don't you think, Kat?"

I stared at him, mouth open. Why was he talking like a news reporter?

"Uh . . . sure?"

"According to this story, Ana was really shy around the media before her diagnosis," Oscar went on. "She loved going to her mom's shows, but she hated the attention she got."

"Well, some people don't like having cameras shoved in their faces." I couldn't help shooting Jess a quick glare, and I heard Dad stifle a laugh. Jess waved at him to be quiet, although I could see she was smiling, too.

"And some people love it." Oscar batted his eyelashes at the camera, and I groaned. Overhead, Mi Jin's shoulders were shaking with silent laughter. "Anyway, I read that Flavia once told off a bunch of reporters after a concert because they were harassing Ana. After that, she stopped bringing Ana to her shows, and she even turned down a European tour."

"You mean before Ana got sick?" I asked. Oscar hadn't mentioned that part when he'd translated for me earlier.

He nodded. "Her manager was really annoyed about it," he said. "But Flavia made it clear that Ana took priority over everything else in her life. Then when Ana got sick, her mom basically gave up everything for her."

I nodded, studying the picture. "I wonder what that's like."

Oscar paused. "What?"

"You know, to have a mom who would . . ." I stopped as I realized what I was saying. *To have a mom who would do that for me.*

A long pause followed, and I could feel everyone staring at me. I gazed at the Ouija board, the letters and numbers suddenly fuzzy. Had that actually come out of my mouth? What was wrong with me? It was one thing to think it, but saying it out loud . . . and with the cameras rolling, too. My heart dropped as I wondered what my dad's expression looked like right now. I didn't dare look up to find out.

Finally, Jess cleared her throat. "All right, let's try the Ouija board." Her tone was uncharacteristically gentle, which just made me feel worse. I nodded, touching my hand to the planchette. After a second, Oscar did the same. Neither of us spoke, and after a few seconds, Mi Jin piped up.

"One of you should talk to Ana out loud," she reminded us.

"Oh yeah." Oscar glanced at me. "Want me to do it?"

"Sure."

We turned our attention back to the board. "Hello, Ana," Oscar said. "I'm Oscar. That's Kat. So . . . how are you?"

I snorted. "She's dead, you dork. How do you think she is?"

"Well, what am I supposed to say?"

"You have to invite her," I said, remembering the way Jamie had contacted Sonja Hillebrandt back in Crimptown. "And we both have to focus on her."

Oscar let out an exaggerated sigh that reminded me strongly of Roland. "Okay. Ana Arias . . . we invite you to join us. Please. You know, unless you're busy."

Gritting my teeth, I tried to focus on Ana. But I was too irritated. This whole thing had been a dumb idea. I didn't want to be on television anyway. I'd probably—

The planchette twitched lightly under my fingers. I

31

could tell immediately that Oscar was trying to move it. Pressing down, I glared at him and shook my head slightly. He rolled his eyes, but the planchette stopped moving after a few seconds.

Focus on Ana, I told myself. But it was a lost cause. Oscar's weird Roland impression was annoying me, the stupid cameras were annoying me, but most of all, I was annoyed with myself. I hardly ever talked about my mother around anyone, much less while I was being recorded. Why had I said that out loud? It's not like I *wanted* my mom to give up everything that made her happy just for me. But what Oscar had said about Ana being Flavia's first priority . . . it was never that way with my mother. Her own happiness had always been her number-one priority, not mine.

"Ana Arias," Oscar repeated. "Are you here? We'd like to ask you a few questions . . ."

Like with this wedding. I was still upset with my mother for leaving last spring, and then for not telling me when she moved back to town. I went over six months without talking to her, and now she expected me to be in her wedding. To wear a pretty dress and make my hair more "stylish" and smile at the camera and basically act more like the daughter she probably wished she'd had in the first—

The planchette lurched across the board, and I gasped. "*Oscar*," I hissed, but he shook his head.

"I'm not doing it!"

After touching the letter *I*, the planchette moved over

32

to *W.* I pressed down again, glaring at Oscar. "Stop screwing around!"

He scowled. "I'm not! It's—" The planchette jerked beneath our fingers, then touched the *A* before zooming over to *N*, and then *T*. I frowned, watching as it moved from letter to letter so fast, it was hard to catch them.

"O," Oscar murmured. "U . . . T."

The planchette fell still, and we looked at each other.

"'I want out?'" I said. "What's that supposed to mean?"

Oscar blinked a few times. Then he patted the ground beneath us and smiled up into Mi Jin's camera. "Sorry, Ana," he said, his annoying new reporter voice going strong. "Digging you up probably isn't the best idea."

"Ha-ha," I said dryly. My skin felt all creepy-crawly and exposed, and I wanted nothing more than to put as much distance between myself and the cameras as possible. I closed my eyes, taking a deep breath. To my intense relief, Jess flipped her camera off and got to her feet.

"Well, that was interesting," she said with a grin. "'I want out,' huh?"

Oscar lifted his shoulders. "That's what Ana said."

Jess eyed him. "Come on, now. You guys really sold that—you even had me going for a second. But it's time to fess up. Which one of you was moving it?"

"I wasn't," Oscar said immediately, and I snorted.

"Yeah, you were."

Mi Jin had lowered her camera, too. "It really didn't look

like either of them were moving it from this angle," she told Jess.

"Because we weren't." Oscar glared at me. "Not me, anyway."

I crossed my arms. "You tried to, and I stopped you. Then I . . . I got distracted, and you started shoving it all over the place!"

"Kat, I swear I—"

"Okay!" Jess interrupted. "If Mi Jin says it looked legit, that's good enough for me. Let's get a few closing comments, and we'll wrap this up." Apparently my despair showed on my face, because Jess took pity on me. "Oscar, why don't you do this one, since Kat introduced the story. Here, let's move back over to Flavia's grave . . ."

Oscar followed her and Mi Jin without looking at me, but I was too relieved to be away from the cameras to feel guilty. Dad walked over to me, hands in his pockets. We stood there silently for a few minutes.

"I suck at this," I said quietly.

Dad smiled. "Nope. Pretty much the opposite, actually. You did a great job."

"Maybe with the research," I admitted. "But I'm talking about being on camera. I hate it."

"You might hate it," Dad said slowly. "But that doesn't mean you're bad at it."

I wrinkled my nose. "I guess we'll find out when this goes online. Can you, um . . ." I fixed my gaze on my shoes, my face growing warm. "Can you make sure Jess edits out that thing I said about, um . . ."

"I will."

"Thanks," I said to my feet. Dad didn't say anything else, and I had the feeling he was waiting to see if I wanted to talk about it. A few seconds passed with nothing but the sound of Oscar talking in the background. Then I blurted out:

"Aren't you mad that Mom's already getting married again?"

Dad exhaled like he'd been holding his breath forever. "No," he said at last, and I looked up.

"Seriously?" I couldn't keep the skepticism from my voice.

He smiled. "Okay, truth? I was. I was hurt, and I was mad. But I'm not anymore."

"Why not?"

"Because, I . . ." Dad hesitated, gazing out over the cemetery. "I wouldn't trade this adventure you and I are on for anything. And I want your mother to be happy, too. Once I realized that, there was no point in feeling hurt and mad anymore. Does that make sense?"

I nodded, because my throat was too tight to respond. It did make sense. It really did.

But I was still hurt. I was still mad. And maybe it made me a terrible daughter, but I still didn't want to be a part of my mother's wedding.

Post (draft): Flavia and Ana Arias
Publish? Yes/No

" JUST publish it already, for the love," Oscar pleaded.
Instead, I moved the cursor over to the video again.

"I just want to watch it one more time."

He moaned loudly, but stopped the second it began playing. I had to admit, Jess and the others had done an amazing job editing our video. It started out with about half a minute of exploring the cemetery while one of Flavia Arias's songs, a slow, haunting ballad, played in the background. My explanation of her story came next. We'd watched this video seven times already, but my stomach still squirmed uncomfortably when I suddenly appeared on the screen. (*Flash!* Sickening Strapless.)

Of course, I wasn't actually wearing a dress. Video-me wore a new T-shirt Grandma had bought me the day after Thanksgiving: black, with *Frankenstein Say Relax* in neon green. The letters kind of glowed in the dark.

I didn't look nearly as nervous as I remembered feeling,

either. And I did sound like I knew what I was talking about, so that was cool. The Ouija part came next, and Oscar leaned forward, watching himself so intently, I almost laughed.

Jess had edited out the part where I'd started talking about my mother, thankfully. Pretty much everything else was there. The video switched angles a few times, then stayed on Mi Jin's overhead shot when the planchette started flying around the Ouija board. I had to admit, it did look legit.

The last part was Oscar speculating about what the message from Ana could mean. *"She loved her mother's songs, but she hated the fame that came with them,"* Oscar said, looking straight into the camera. *"'I want out' doesn't make much sense as some sort of message from her ghost . . . but it could be an echo of her consciousness. On the next episode of* Passport to Paranormal, *we'll be investigating the site of a residual haunting. This message from Ana could be something similar. Stay tuned to Kat's blog for more about where we're filming next, here in Salvador. And if you have any theories about Ana Arias, we'd love to hear about them in the comments!"*

As much as I hated to admit it, Oscar's weird reporter voice worked. He was really charismatic on camera, especially compared to me. It made me even more self-conscious. (Not that I'd ever tell him that.)

"That was my idea, to plug the next episode at the end of the video," Oscar said. "Jess loved it."

I pressed my lips together. "I know. You told me last night. Twice."

"I heard her telling Roland that she changed her mind about us," Oscar went on as if he hadn't heard me. "She thinks Fright TV is right, that adding us is really going to help the show."

"Somehow I doubt Roland agrees," I said, touching the trackpad on Dad's laptop. "Okay, here we go." I clicked *Yes*, and a second later, a new post appeared on my blog. "Ugh. It's up."

Oscar finally tore his gaze from the screen and looked hard at me. "Seriously, Kat," he said. "Why do you hate this so much? It's not like you to get freaked out about . . . well, anything."

I shrugged. "I don't know. Maybe it's because I'm a photographer. I just like being behind the camera, not in front of it." There was more to it than that, but I didn't know how to explain the way my skin crawled when the cameras were filming me, like my skeleton was ready to leap out of my body and make a run for it. "Anyway, why do you like it so much? You're way more into this than I thought you'd be."

Oscar's eyes flickered to the screen. "It's just . . . it's fun, that's all." He clicked the refresh button and scrolled down to the comments, which still said *0*.

"We literally published it ten seconds ago," I told him with a grin. "I'm thinking people will want to actually watch it before they leave comments."

"We should put a link in the *P2P* forums!" Oscar said suddenly, pulling the laptop closer. "I'll do that right now."

I got to my feet and grabbed a pen and the black-and-white composition notebook Dad had bought for me this morning. "Let me know when you're done, okay? I need to write that post about the next episode."

"'Kay." His eyes stayed glued to the forums as I headed into the hall. I found Sam in the lobby, reading a magazine. Roland lounged in an armchair nearby, scribbling in a book titled *1,001 Brain-Twisting Crossword Puzzles*. He arched an eyebrow when I sat next to Sam on the sofa and opened my notebook.

"Excuse me, ma'am," Roland drawled. "All interviews with Sam Sumners must be arranged through his manager."

Sam's brow furrowed. "I don't have a manager."

"You do, actually," Roland said, tapping his pencil against his mouth. "I hired one. He's incredible."

"Who is it?"

"Me." Roland squinted down at his book. "Hey, do either of you know a four-letter word that means 'really terrible at crossword puzzles'? Pretty sure it starts with a *Q* and ends with . . . um, also *Q*."

I snickered. "Nope, sorry. And I'm not interviewing Sam. He said he'd tell me about this waterfall we're investigating so I can write a blog post. Is that okay with his manager?"

Roland pretended to consider it. "Approved, I suppose," he said at last. "Man, Jess wasn't kidding about you, was she?"

"What?"

"She said you're a natural journalist." Roland wrinkled his nose as he erased something on his puzzle. "I watched the cemetery video. It wasn't awful."

"It was really good," Sam told me seriously. "I'm impressed you were able to contact Ana so quickly."

"Thanks," I said. "If it was really Ana."

Sam tilted his head. "You don't think it was her?"

"I don't know." I didn't want to tell him I still didn't entirely believe Oscar hadn't been pushing the planchette. "It wasn't like when we contacted Sonja, that's all. I was kind of distracted."

"Why?" He studied me intently. Sam had a way of making people spill their guts, and I was starting to figure out why. He actually *listened*. Unlike most people, who only half-listen because they're trying to figure out how they're going to respond to you.

"Because of the stupid cameras."

Sam smiled sympathetically. "I understand. I was uncomfortable with the cameras during our first few episodes, but now I barely even notice them when we visit a haunted site."

"To be fair, you barely notice other living humans when we visit a haunted site," Roland pointed out.

Sam ignored this. "You'll get used to it, Kat. I promise. It's just stage fright."

I blinked. Stage fright? Seriously? But I'd never had that

before. Not in the school play in fourth grade, when I played the Evil Queen to Trish's Snow White. Not last year during class elections, when I'd moderated a debate in the cafeteria between Mark and the other class-president candidates. Sure, I'd been a little nervous, but in the fun kind of way.

This camera thing? Not fun, and I didn't *want* to get used to being on TV.

But I didn't say any of that to Sam. I just smiled.

"Thanks. Anyway . . . what's the story behind this waterfall?"

Almost an hour later, I returned to my room with several pages of notes. I'd never really thought about this part of Dad's work before. Back when he hosted a morning talk show called *Rise and Shine, Ohio!* I just thought his job meant sitting in front of a camera, talking about the news, and making jokes. It was definitely not a career I'd ever be interested in. But this—doing research and "finding the story," as Jess put it—this part I actually liked. The whole time Sam had been talking, I was mentally writing my blog post. I even found myself planning out how I'd want to film the episode, if I were in charge. On the not-terrifying side of the cameras, of course.

Oscar was gone, and he'd left Dad's laptop open on the desk. I sat down and clicked over to my blog. "Thirty-seven comments," I mumbled. "Woo."

EdieM: This is FANTASTIC! So proud of you, KitKat.

trishhhh: !!!!!!!!!!!!!!!!!!!!!!!!!!!!

MARK: Nice! Love your shirt, btw.

Maytrix: Wow, excellent mini episode! Oscar, you crack me up. Can't wait to see you guys on the next episode!

JamieBaggins: As an official Ouija Master, I proclaim this to be outstanding Ouija-ing.

skEllen: OMG THIS IS AMAZING!!! OSCAR IS SUCH A CUTIE! I HOPE YOU DO LOTS MORE OF THESE!!!!!1!!!

AntiSimon: Kat, this is really great! Thanks for sharing this story about Flavia and Ana with us. Oscar is too funny!

Heyyyyley: This. Is. So. COOL.

YourCohortInCrime: Wow, you could've at least tried not to make it obvious you were moving that planchette. Cheap stunt.

presidentskroob: what a tragic story

I scrolled through the comments, smiling when I recognized some of the fans from the *P2P* forums. Quite a few thought Oscar and I had faked the Ouija thing, but whatever. Some people would always be skeptics, no matter what.

There were a few anonymous comments, and over a dozen from people I didn't know, either from real life or the forums. I'd nearly reached the bottom when one caught my eye.

kbold04: did u think kat wuz a boy at first? i did lol

I read the comment several times, and a strange, sour feeling sprouted in my stomach and wormed its way up to my heart. Numbly, I scrolled back up to the video and clicked *Play*, then skipped through the first minute or so until I saw myself on the screen. I clicked *Pause* and leaned forward, scrutinizing everything about my appearance.

Between the camera angle and the lack of light, it was impossible to see the super-short ponytail sticking out of the back of my head unless I turned. My black Frankenstein T-shirt was pretty shapeless—not that I had much shape to fill out a more revealing top, anyway—and I had on yellow board shorts and flip-flops. I never wore make-up, but that shouldn't matter. Plenty of girls didn't. And my face was . . . just my face.

I chewed my lip, staring hard at the screen. *Did* I look like a boy?

"There's nothing wrong with being a girly girl, Kat."

My mother had said that at least a hundred times last week. It was like after six months of not speaking, she had to let out all the criticism she'd been storing up. Every time she said it, it took everything I had not to retort, *I know there's nothing wrong with that. There's nothing wrong with being me, either.*

But staring at kbold04's comment, I started to wonder

if maybe I *was* wrong, after all.

"Hey, Kat!"

Gasping, I swiveled in my chair to find Mi Jin in the doorway. "Oh!" My voice came out kind of squeaky. "Hi! What's up?"

"I was just heading downstairs to get some dinner and saw your door open," Mi Jin said, glancing at my laptop. Her face lit up when she saw the video. "Oh hey—you posted it! Any comments yet?"

"Um . . . yeah."

I stood up and went to sit on the bed so Mi Jin could read through the comments. "Aw, Jamie and Hailey are so funny," she said, smiling. "I can't wait to see them next week . . . Heh, that Cohort dude from the forums thinks you guys faked the Ouija thing, what a shocker . . ."

My heart pounded faster as I waited for her to see it. A few seconds later, the smile faded from her face.

"Ugh, freaking trolls," she muttered. "Loser. Do you want me to . . ." Trailing off, Mi Jin squinted at me. "Kat? You okay?"

I shrugged. "Yeah, fine." My eyes felt dangerously hot, so I fixed my attention on the bedspread.

"Hey." Mi Jin scooted the chair over until she was right in front of me. "That comment didn't get to you, did it? Kat, that's just a stupid troll."

"I know."

"They say mean stuff just for fun."

"I know."

"You're one of the most confident, awesome kids I've ever met," Mi Jin said. "You and Oscar both. I hate seeing the dumb things people say hurt you guys like this."

I wrinkled my nose. "What are you talking about? The fans all love him."

"I meant . . . never mind." Leaning forward, Mi Jin nudged my knees with hers. "Look. *Are* you a girl?"

"Yeah," I said, startled.

"Then you look like a girl," Mi Jin said firmly. She scooted back over to the laptop and started clicking. "You look like you, and you're the only person who gets to decide who that is. The end. I'm deleting that stupid comment."

As I watched her, the knot in my chest loosened a little bit. "Thanks."

"Anytime." Closing the laptop, she faced me again. "Did I ever tell you about the time I cosplayed as Moondragon at Comic-Con when I was sixteen?"

"Who?"

Her eyes widened. "Moondragon! Avengers? Guardians of the Galaxy? Argh—okay, I have some comics you need to read. Mandatory." She nodded decisively. "Anyway. So I put together a pretty decent costume: green bathing suit, green boots, green cape with a really high collar. I got a bald cap, because Moondragon is bald, right? But it looked super fake. So I shaved my head."

My mouth fell open. "You did?"

"Yep," Mi Jin said proudly. "My parents were *furious*, and

I couldn't figure out why. I mean, it's my head. Moondragon was bald, and I wanted to look like her. Even my best friend was like, 'But people will think you're a boy!'"

"And it didn't bother you?" I asked.

Mi Jin shrugged. "Nope. Why should it? Their mistake, not mine. I liked how it looked, honestly." She paused, running her fingers through her hair. "Maybe I should go back to that. My mom would *freak*."

I giggled. "My mom always hated my costumes, too. I was Dracula when I was seven, and Grandma helped me make my costume. It was *awesome*. A bunch of neighbors didn't even recognize me! I remember Mrs. Vesky down the street saying, 'And who's this little boy?' Drove my mom nuts, but I loved it. Isn't the point of a costume to fool people into thinking you're someone else?"

"Totally!" Mi Jin beamed.

"Elena's going through a princess phase," I told her. "My mom loves it."

"Who?"

I immediately regretted bringing her up. "My mom's fiancé's daughter. Hey, want to get some dinner?"

Mi Jin studied me for a few seconds before responding. "Sure, yeah."

I stood and headed to the door, saying a silent thanks that Mi Jin hadn't pressed me to talk more about Elena. What she said about not letting other people decide who you are made a whole lot of sense. Besides, Grandma liked makeup and dresses and all that, but she never, ever made me feel bad for not liking them, too.

Still, I couldn't stop thinking about that comment, and I couldn't help wondering if there'd be more . . . especially if I ended up on television after all.

CHAPTER FOUR
THE ONLY THING MISSING IS A MANIAC WITH A CHAINSAW

Post: The Lost Campers of Chapada Diamantina

Tomorrow morning, the *P2P* crew is heading to Chapada Diamantina National Park, about a five-hour drive from Salvador. We're going to camp out overnight near a waterfall where three teens died in the summer of 1974.

According to the locals my dad interviewed yesterday, this group of friends went camping the weekend after school let out. When they packed up to leave, they realized they'd lost their hiking trail map. They tried to find their way, but they kept circling back to the waterfall. Soon they ran out of food.

It was weeks before authorities found their bodies. They also found their footprints circling the area over and over again. Ever since then, other campers have reported feeling a strong sense of fear and panic near the waterfall. Some even claim to hear the frantic whispers of the teens as they wander through the trees, lost.

Sam believes the waterfall might be an example of a residual haunting. That's when the emotions of the people who died are trapped in an energy field and the event is "replayed" again and again, as though it's on a loop. If he's right, that means we won't actually see the ghosts of the lost campers, since this type of haunting is like a record of their feelings—their actual spirits won't be present. Hopefully we'll find out one way or the other tonight.

Also, big news! Oscar and I are officially joining the cast of

P2P, starting with this episode. We're both really excited about it, and we hope you are, too!

ABOUT an hour into the drive, I was ready to scream. Oscar would not stop talking about what the fans were writing about him. He'd stayed up so late reading the *P2P* forums last night that Lidia told us she'd had to literally drag him out of bed this morning. There were new threads just to discuss the newest cast members, me and Oscar. I had already made a silent vow not to read them anymore. Which would be pretty easy to stick to in a national park with no reception.

Oscar, on the other hand, was *obsessed*. Probably because the fans already totally loved him. Maybe I thought his reporter personality was annoying, but apparently it was effective.

"Did anyone say anything bad?" I asked him at one point, and he shrugged.

"A few thought the Ouija part was fake."

"Yeah, but I mean . . ." I fidgeted in my seat. "Well, there was this comment on my blog yesterday. Mi Jin deleted it, but . . ."

Oscar stared at me. "What did it say?"

"Just . . . this rude comment about how I looked like a boy or something," I said as offhandedly as possible.

"Oh that."

I turned to him. "Wait, you saw it?"

"Yeah." Oscar shrugged. "Just a troll, right? They show

up in the forums, too, sometimes. It's not a big deal."

"I guess, yeah."

I looked out the window, feeling a little stung. Oscar had been bullied before, after all. Being tormented by your friends was obviously way worse than having one dumb troll say something mean about you online, but still. I guess I'd figured he'd be a little more sympathetic.

Or maybe I really was making too big a deal of this.

"Not sure *Camp Half Hell* was the best thing to watch right before camping," Lidia mused, grabbing a bunch of cables out of the back of the van.

"Think of it as training in case things go wrong," I told her. "Basically, don't do anything the counselors do, and you probably won't die."

"And stay close to Kat," Oscar added as he zipped his iPad up in its case. "Maybe her grandma taught her how to defend herself against a serial killer with a curling iron."

Mi Jin hopped out of the van wearing a gigantic backpack. "Oscar Bettencourt," she said sternly. "You know I love being pranked, but if you come at me with a curling iron at any point tonight, I am not responsible for any serious bodily harm that may befall you."

"Aw, come on . . ." Picking up his bag, Oscar followed Mi Jin down the dirt path. Dad and Jess, both weighed down with camera equipment, were already up ahead with our guides. Brenda and Hugo, who ran a small tour business in a nearby town, had told us the waterfall would be at least an hour's hike from where we parked. Roland and Sam weren't far behind, each carrying two extra-long duffel bags containing our tents. I helped Lidia get the last of our supplies out of the van, and we set off after the others.

Most of the hike was uphill. The incline wasn't all that steep, but after half an hour, my calves had started to ache. Then we stepped out of the trees, and I forgot about my sore legs.

"Wow." On either side of us, grassy hills rose up and up until they were vertical, turning into rocky cliffs that towered overhead. The sun hung low in the sky, causing the stone to glow gold and orange.

"Gorgeous," Lidia said happily, readjusting her backpack straps as we walked. "Mmm, it feels so good to be outside. Jess spent Thanksgiving with us in Oregon, and she yelled at me when I so much as got out of bed."

"Well, you did look pretty sick the last time we saw you," I told her. Which was putting it kindly, to be honest. After the whole Emily disaster at Daems, Lidia had told us the last thing she remembered was setting up in the mess hall. Then she woke up to Jess giving her CPR and figured she'd passed out. She definitely did *not* remember when Red Leer took over her body, forcing her to run from cell to cell and free all the ghostly prisoners. And giving Oscar and me a pretty good scare while she was at it.

"True," Lidia agreed. "But I'm pretty tough. I mean, I was possessed all that time between Crimptown and Daems, and I managed."

I glanced at her. "But you didn't know it, right?"

"That I was possessed? Not exactly." Lidia frowned, toying with the locket on her necklace. "It's hard to explain. I didn't have blackouts, but there were these moments where I'd see something, or *feel* something, that wasn't real. Like the day we left Rotterdam—I looked out at the waterfront and saw a ship way out on the ocean. A really *old* ship. Then I blinked and it was gone. A little hallucination, courtesy of Red Leer."

"Whoa."

"Yeah." Lidia shook her head. "The weirdest part was when I saw it, I felt this . . . this *connection* to it. Like it was my ship, and I wanted nothing more than to be on it, to just sail out into the ocean and never look back." She sighed, wiping the sweat from her forehead. "Anyway. At least now I know the signs of possession firsthand, right? Not many people can say that."

"I guess," I said. "You have your heart medicine, right?" Lidia had been born with a condition that meant she needed to be fitted with a pacemaker. Since manipulating electricity took less energy for ghosts, it was her pacemaker that made her easier for them to possess.

Lidia let out a short laugh. "Yes, and just so you know, Jess and Oscar have been checking to make sure I take it every day. Incessantly. Between them and Sam, sometimes I feel like no one trusts me to take care of myself anymore."

She said it lightly, but I noticed her forehead crease a little. "Sam, really?" I asked. "He doesn't seem like the nagging type."

"He's the one who found this site," Lidia said. "He insisted on investigating a residual haunting because there's no risk for me. These ghosts can't interact because they're not real ghosts, they're just recordings. An echo."

"Huh."

"I agreed because this waterfall does have an interesting story," Lidia went on. "But I set up the Buenos Aires investigation. Jess and Sam weren't too happy with my choice."

"It's a church, right?" I asked.

"Right. But the story is actually in the catacombs under the church. They're haunted by a nun." Lidia grinned at me. "A nun who was supposedly possessed by a demon over a century ago."

"Awesome!" I exclaimed. "Kind of like *Return to the Asylum*. Although I guess I can see why they're worried about you, after what happened with Red Leer."

Lidia sighed. "I know. But I'm thirty-two years old. I've been ghost hunting pretty much since I was seven, when my brother and I first heard all the stories about how our town's lighthouse was haunted. I understand everyone's concern, but I can take care of myself." Taking off her sunglasses, she squinted ahead. "Looks like we're heading off the path."

Hugo led the way down a much narrower path into the trees, Dad and Jess right behind him. Roland followed, then Sam and Oscar. Brenda smiled at Lidia and me as she waited for us to pass her so she could bring up the rear.

This path was a fairly steep decline, but the thick roots and weeds made it more strenuous than going uphill. No one spoke much, although Roland kept whistling the theme song from *The Addams Family* until Jess begged him to stop.

"Blame Kat," he called over his shoulder. "Her shirt got it stuck in my head."

"W-W-W-D?" said Brenda from behind me, reading the back of my shirt. "What does it mean?"

I turned so she could see the front. "*What Would Wednesday Do . . .* ow!"

"Careful!" She grabbed my arm to steady me as I kicked away the bramble that had scratched my calf. After that, I focused harder on the climb down. Twenty minutes later, the distant sound of a waterfall reached my ears, quickly growing to a roar. I pulled the Elapse from my pocket and flipped it on as Brenda helped us over the last few rocks.

"Nice." I stood on the last rock, snapping several photos of the falls. Water gushed from an opening at the top of a fairly short cliff into a large, crystal-clear pool. Through the mist, I could just make out a small cave behind the falls. The surrounding banks were wide enough to set up camp before the ground turned steep, like a circle of mini cliffs enclosing the area. I could see a few other paths snaking out and up among the massive trees that grew out of the rocky yellow-brown earth. Overhead, long, twisty branches thick with bright green, leathery leaves reached out to one another over the pool, leaving just a bit of open sky.

Oscar kicked off his shoes and scrambled down the rocks toward the pool. "Hang on!" Lidia called after him. "Let's get this on video."

I made a face, staying on my rock as everyone else made their way to the banks. Jess and Mi Jin pulled their cameras out as soon as they reached the bottom. Oscar waded knee deep into the pool, followed by Roland.

"How is the water?" called Hugo, who was helping Dad set up one of the tents.

"Freezing!" Oscar was already backing out. "Too cold to swim."

"Not if you do it the right way." Hugo grinned, pointing. "Like Brenda."

Everyone looked up to see Brenda standing on a ledge near the waterfall, about halfway up the cliff. She waved before cannonballing into the pool below. Roland stood stock still as the resulting splash covered him. "Thank you for that," he said solemnly when Brenda surfaced, and she laughed.

"*Sem problema.*"

Several minutes passed while Jess and Mi Jin got footage

of everyone else setting up the tents, organizing supplies, and taking turns jumping off the cliff. I was getting some great shots, although with every minute that passed, the pool looked more and more tempting. I was hot and dirty from the hike, and the water was so inviting . . . but coming down off my rock meant being on camera. On *television*. I didn't want to cannonball on TV. I didn't want to do *anything* on TV. If I was already getting criticism about how I looked from trolls on my blog, what would happen when my face was on television?

"Get over it," I told myself, irritated. Oscar was right; this wasn't like me at all. Ignoring the way my stomach had started to churn, I grabbed my bag and climbed off the rock. After tucking my Elapse safely inside, I left the bag near the tent Dad and Hugo had finished setting up and followed Oscar, who was heading back up the steep path to the ledge for what was probably his fifth or sixth jump. When we reached it, he turned to me with a grand gesture.

"Ladies first."

"*Obriga*-da," I said, walking to the edge. The ledge seemed a lot higher from up here. Dad waved to me, and I waved back, grateful Jess was occupied filming Roland and Hugo competing to see who could stand under the waterfall the longest.

"How cold is it, really?" I asked Oscar over my shoulder.

He pushed his sopping-wet bangs out of his eyes. "Cold. Really cold."

"But, like, on a scale of North Pole when the reindeer are frozen solid to Pluto after an asteroid knocks it out of the sun's orbit."

"Hmm." Oscar tapped his chin. "I'd say probably Antarctica, on a glacier, during an ice battle between Elsa and the Abominable Snowman."

"Cool," I said, nodding. "For the record, Elsa would totally win."

"Um, obviously."

As I faced the pool again, a feeling of unease passed over me. Tiny goose bumps broke out on my arms in spite of the heat. I rubbed my arms, frowning. A second later, the sensation was gone.

Taking a deep breath, I jumped. The second or two of free-falling felt incredible. Then I plunged into the pool, and the sharp sting of icy water drove all thoughts from my mind.

A voice screamed in my head, and I exhaled a short burst of bubbles, flailing frantically. I opened my eyes and tilted my head toward what I thought was the surface. Another face stared back at me.

Mine.

I just barely stopped myself from letting out a scream. Instinctively, I reached out, and my hand passed through my eyes, my nose, my mouth, scattering my reflection. A second later, my head broke through the surface.

Sucking in a warm gulp of air, I blinked the freezing water from my eyes. It was a few seconds before the muddled sounds around me turned to recognizable words.

"How's it feel?" Dad was calling from where he stood next to Jess.

"Great!" My voice came out hoarse, and I tried to smile as I floated away from them. I felt kind of silly, letting the sight of my own reflection scare me like that. Even if it was an especially vivid reflection.

Now that the shock had subsided, the water was starting to feel . . . well, it was still freezing. But bearable. Enough so that I could stay put and avoid parading around in front of the cameras in my sopping-wet Wednesday Addams shirt.

Treading water, I hummed the theme from *Jaws* under my breath. *Just when you thought it was safe to go back in the water . . .*

The unease swept over me again. It was the same feeling I got during the first scene of a horror movie, where everyone looks totally happy, moments before something gruesome happens. I shook it off, but the water suddenly felt much colder. I watched as the others made their way out of the pool and joined Dad and Jess, who were opening the coolers of food. "Let's make this a quick dinner," I heard Jess say. "We need to get rolling."

Sighing, I forced myself to swim toward them. Like it or not, it was almost time to start shooting my first-ever television episode.

Nighttime totally transformed our campsite. It was a kind of darkness I'd never experienced outdoors; it even seemed to swallow the beam from my (admittedly weak) flashlight. Brenda and Hugo had provided us with maps that marked where the campers' footsteps had been found, and we were trying to retrace their path and figure out how they'd managed to circle around and around and never find their way out. Already, Sam had claimed to be experiencing "an intense sense of anxiety and despair." Roland had responded by offering him anti-diarrhea medicine. ("Sometimes despair is really just the runs.")

While Oscar hovered around Jess and Mi Jin, cracking jokes for the cameras every five seconds, I trailed behind everyone. I thought my Elapse was a good pretense—after all, I wanted to get shots of the group trekking around for my blog. But after half an hour, Jess pulled me aside.

"How about joining Oscar up at the front for a little bit?" she asked kindly. I wrinkled my nose.

"Do I have to?"

Jess studied me for a few seconds. "The thing is, the network made it clear they don't want one kid tagging along with a bunch of adults. They want clips of the two of you together. Like the graveyard mini episode. Which they loved, by the way."

"They did?"

"Yup." She smiled. "It pretty much sealed the deal as far as you two becoming cast members. Look, try to stop thinking about the cameras so much, okay? Just relax and be yourself."

"I'll try." *Although Oscar isn't being himself on camera,* I couldn't help adding in my head as I followed her. I felt guilty even thinking it, but his weird new über-charming on-camera persona was driving me nuts. Maybe the fans loved it, but I preferred the real Oscar.

After consulting the maps again, Brenda and Hugo led us through a cluster of large rocks. The path twisted and turned like a maze. When we finally got out, I was pretty sure we were heading back in the direction of the pool— circling around just like the campers had done. It was easy to see how they'd gotten so lost.

Several minutes later, we were all huddled around a tree with thick, knotted roots twisting up out of the ground. Sam knelt next to it, placed his palm on the bark, and closed his eyes. "One of them tripped here," he said gravely. "She hit her head . . . possibly a concussion." Blinking, he stared around as if he expected to spot the lost campers behind us.

A wave of anxiety washed over me, so strong my knees almost buckled. I stepped back quickly, praying Jess and Mi Jin wouldn't notice. They kept their cameras focused on Dad and Lidia, whose EMF meters had apparently started spiking. But Oscar glanced over at me, frowning.

"What's wrong?"

"Nothing," I whispered quickly. "Just a little dizzy."

His eyes narrowed. "Dizzy? Wait, are you sensing . . .

whatever Sam's sensing? The campers? You should tell Jess, this is—"

"No," I snapped, straightening up. "It's not that. I'm fine, I just . . . I have to pee."

"Does having to pee usually make you dizzy?"

I glared at him. "Ha-ha."

"Kat, this is the whole point of the show," Oscar said in a low voice. "It's a paranormal investigation, and you're sensing something paranormal. So just . . . just get over your stupid camera thing already so we can tell Jess about it."

If my heart hadn't been jackhammering in my chest, that might have hurt my feelings. Instead, it made me angry. So I turned my back on Oscar and walked over to Brenda.

"I have to pee," I told her, doing my best to keep my voice from shaking. "I'm not allowed to go off alone, so can you take me?"

"Of course!"

I caught Dad's eye and pointed to Brenda, so he'd see I had a chaperone. Then we quietly slipped away through the trees.

"I'm glad you asked me," Brenda whispered, smiling. "I have to go too, but I didn't want to interrupt the filming." We emerged from the bushes back at the pool, and she pointed to the far end. "I'll be right over there when you're done, okay?"

I nodded. "Thanks."

After she walked away, I moved closer to the waterfall. The cold mist mingled with the sweat on my face. My heart had finally slowed to a normal rate, but my stomach still twinged with anxiety. For a second, I wondered if Oscar was right; maybe this *was* what Sam had felt. Maybe I was sensing the emotions of the residual haunting. But I'd been nervous around the cameras back in the graveyard, too. My "stage fright," or whatever it was, was getting worse.

I could see the opening to the cave behind the waterfall now. Instinctively, my fingers grazed my pocket, where my camera was tucked away. I felt guilty for letting Jess down, sneaking off like this right after she'd encouraged me to participate more. The least I could do was contribute some cool photos. I might not be good on camera, but I was good behind one.

Climbing up on a wide ledge about a foot off the ground, I edged around the rock and stepped inside the cave. It was shallow enough that I could see the back, but too dark to make out how high up it went. It was fairly eerie, too. Had the campers explored this cave before they'd gotten lost?

Flipping on my Elapse, I took a few more steps to the center of the cave and started taking pictures. It was too dark in there to bother with framing, and Brenda was probably finished by now, so I had to be quick.

Flash. Flash. Flash. I turned in a full circle, then took a few shots of the ceiling. The sudden brightness left spots dancing in my vision.

Blinking, I squinted at my display screen and scrolled through the pictures. The flash gave the rocky interior an orange hue, exposing every bump and crack. But there was a pattern to it. It took a few seconds for my brain to register what I was seeing. Three words, scratched all over the walls, even at the top of the cave where no one could possibly reach:

I WANT OUT

CHAPTER FIVE
ONE CAMPER ENTERS THE CAVE, BUT HOW MANY WILL COME OUT?

P2P WIKI
Entry: "Thoughtography"
[Last edited by AntiSimon]

Thoughtography is a process in which a person projects their thoughts (images, words) onto photos or videos. Sometimes referred to as psychic photography or videography.

NUMBLY, I groped for the small flashlight clipped to the waistband of my shorts. When I finally grasped it, I shined it around on the walls. No words, just rock. I stared back down at the Elapse screen, a chill creeping up my spine. How was this possible?

I stumbled out of the cave and hopped off the ledge, fighting the urge to run. I started heading to the far side of the pool, but a rustling noise stopped me in my tracks. Freezing, I stared hard at the bushes, which were perfectly still.

"Brenda?" I whispered. No response.

Once again, fear and panic hit me like a gust of strong wind.

It took a massive effort to keep my feet planted when all I wanted to do was sprint through the trees and get as far away from this place as possible. Logically, I knew this must be the effect of the residual haunting, and there was nothing to be afraid of. But I sensed something, like a presence. If I weren't so terrified, I might have laughed at myself for thinking like Sam.

The bush twitched, and my heart skipped a beat. Had I imagined that? Pulse thrumming in my ears, I flipped the Elapse to video mode and started to record. If I could get footage of something, anything paranormal, maybe it would make up for how awkward I'd been earlier when Jess tried to film me. My hands shook slightly as I kept the camera trained across the pond, my eyes flickering back and forth between the bush and the screen.

A moment later, a transparent wisp of a figure slid out from between the trees.

I took an involuntary step forward, and then other, until the water lapped at my feet. For a moment, my panic subsided, replaced with wonder. Was this one of the campers?

The figure stood so still, I briefly thought I'd imagined it. Then it shifted slightly, tilting its head, and something about its shape and the way it moved made me suddenly sure of two things.

This ghost was a girl. And she was looking right at me.

When she lifted her hand and waved, I gasped and dropped my camera.

Splash!

"No, no, no!" I hissed, kneeling down and swiping it out

of the water. But it was too late. Clutching my soaking-wet Elapse, I stared across the pool. The girl had vanished.

"Kat?"

I barely stopped myself from screaming as I whirled around to see Brenda waving to me from the far end of the pool.

"Coming!" I managed to choke out. I cast one last glance across the water, but the ghost was gone.

"Give it here."

Mi Jin snatched my poor Elapse from my hands and knelt on the ground. I watched as she pulled a small Tupperware container from her backpack and popped the lid off.

"Is that rice?" Oscar asked, leaning closer.

Nodding, Mi Jin placed my camera inside. "Uncooked rice," she explained, covering the camera completely before snapping the lid back on. "It draws the moisture out. No guarantees, but I've saved a few phones from water damage this way."

"So it might still work?" I asked hopefully.

"Possibly," Mi Jin replied. "We'll find out in the morning— it usually takes several hours for the rice to do its thing."

"Thank you," I told her, the knot in my chest loosening slightly. That Elapse wasn't just the coolest (and most expensive) thing I owned, but it had also been a gift from Grandma. I couldn't believe I'd possibly destroyed it already.

"Mi Jin, will you take over with Sam and Roland?" Jess asked. "I need to talk to Kat for a sec."

Dad and I stayed behind while Mi Jin and Oscar headed down the trail to rejoin the rest of the crew. When Jess turned to me, I glanced at her camera and my stomach sank. And sure enough:

"Would you mind explaining what you saw?" Jess shouldered her camera. "Hopefully we can save your footage, but I'd like to hear about it in your own words, too."

"How about this," Dad said, before I could respond. "Just tell me about it." He gave Jess a little nod, then smiled at me. "So, Kat. Wandered off again, hmm?"

I rolled my eyes. "I was with Brenda the whole time. Except for when she was peeing, because, ew. Privacy."

Dad laughed. "Fair enough. So tell me about what you saw."

I WANT OUT. I saw it in my mind, three words carved all over the interior of the cave. But I didn't want to tell Dad, or anyone, about that. Not when there was a good chance I'd lost those photos forever.

"I was by the waterfall," I said slowly. "I thought I heard something in the bushes, so I turned on my camera. And I felt . . . afraid. Like I felt *their* fear."

"Their?"

"The campers," I explained, feeling stupid. "It's like it wasn't my fear I was feeling."

Jess stepped closer, and I cringed. My skin started

doing that crawly thing again.

"And then you dropped your camera?" Dad asked.

"Yeah, I . . ."

I didn't want to say anything about the ghost, the girl who'd looked at me. It didn't make any sense. This was a residual haunting. A memory. But this ghost had *waved* at me; there was nothing residual about her. Without my camera, I didn't have proof. I'd sound like I was either making it up or so spooked that I'd started seeing things.

"I slipped on a rock," I said at last. "That's when I dropped my camera. So I found Brenda and we came back here."

"Anything else?" Dad asked encouragingly, and I knew he wanted me to give Jess a little more to work with. Oscar probably would've told this story in a much more entertaining way than me.

I shrugged. "Nope. That's it."

Jess lowered her camera. "Thanks, Kat."

"Sure."

Dad put his arm around me, and the three of us headed down the trail to find the others. I couldn't stop thinking about the girl ghost, and *I WANT OUT* carved all over the cave. The same words from our Ouija séance in the graveyard. Why would the same message appear in two different . . .

I inhaled sharply, then disguised it as a cough when Dad glanced at me. When we reached the rest of the crew, I pulled Oscar aside.

"Do you swear you didn't fake the Ouija thing?"

Oscar rolled his eyes. "For the hundredth time, I didn't. Why?"

"Because, I . . ." Trailing off, I studied Oscar for a second. Part of me really wanted to tell him my theory so he could tell me if I sounded like a nutjob. But he'd probably drag me over to Jess so we could talk about it on camera. More airtime for him.

"Never mind."

Too early the next morning, I woke up to find a massive mosquito making a meal out of my elbow. "Away, tiny vampire," I muttered, flicking it. Next to me, Dad let out an extra-loud snore. After swapping the *Halloween* shirt I'd slept in for a clean *Night of the Living Dead*, I crept quietly out of the tent.

Yawning, I squinted around our campsite. We'd finished our investigation around 2:30 a.m. and agreed there was nothing wrong with getting a late start in the morning. It looked like almost everyone was still asleep. No sign of Oscar, but I spotted Brenda up on the ledge we'd used as a diving board yesterday, laying with her legs dangling off the edge as she read a book. Roland and Sam were sitting on a rock on the other side of the pool. At the sight of their thermoses and the cooler, my stomach rumbled loudly.

"What's for breakfast?" I asked when I reached them, climbing up to sit next to Sam. Roland took a long swig from his thermos before responding.

"Coffee."

"And?"

"And more coffee." He held out the thermos, and I wrinkled my nose.

"And granola bars," Sam said, handing me the box. "There's fruit in the cooler, too."

"Thanks." I unwrapped a granola bar, thinking. I needed to tell someone what I'd seen last night. Normally, I'd go to Dad. But last night as I pretended to sleep, I'd realized I couldn't tell him. He would probably be pretty freaked out that I was seeing things. He was already worried that I was traumatized from the whole Emily experience. What if he thought I couldn't handle ghost hunting anymore, and he sent me back to Ohio? To live with *Mom*?

Nope.

I cleared my throat. "Okay, here's the deal. Something happened last night, and I need to tell someone. But you *cannot* tell anyone else. Especially Jess or my dad."

Roland leaned away, cradling his thermos. "This isn't *girl* stuff, is it?" he asked, eyes wide with mock horror.

I snorted. "No. Ghost stuff."

Sam perked up. "We won't tell anyone. Go ahead."

So I told them everything: the message in the cave, the ghost across the pool. How I could tell she was a girl. How she waved at me.

"So do you think it's Ana Arias?" I finished, crumpling

my granola-bar wrapper. "Is it possible she followed us here after Oscar and I contacted her?"

Sam studied me thoughtfully. "That does seem to be the most likely explanation. Although I have to admit, I've been puzzling over Ana's message since I watched your video. She's at rest next to her mother . . . I don't understand what she could mean by *I want out.*" He gazed over at the cave, frowning slightly. "If she followed you all this way, she must feel truly unsettled to leave her mother behind."

"Well . . ." I'd given this a lot of thought last night, but I couldn't decide if it sounded stupid or not. "When we went to the graveyard, there were lots of flowers at Flavia's and Ana's graves. Fresh ones. Ever since people found out about Ana, they've been visiting. Maybe . . . maybe Ana doesn't like the attention. I mean, she hated dealing with reporters because of her mom being a celebrity, and Flavia's death has made her famous all over again. So *I want out* could mean Ana just wants to get away from all that."

Sam blinked a few times, a slow smile spreading across his face. "Kat Sinclair," he said. "You're really getting the hang of this. Perhaps you have a future as a medium."

"Er . . . thanks, I think." I glanced at Roland, whose face was scrunched up all weird. "What?"

Sam turned to Roland, too. "You have to admit her theory is plausible."

"Mmmf." Roland shook his head, lips pressed together even tighter. I sighed.

"You think I'm nuts?"

Exhaling loudly, Roland screwed the lid back on his thermos. "No. It *is* a good theory. But it's not the most likely one."

I waited. "Well?"

"You're not gonna like it . . ." When I just glared at him in response, he shrugged. "All right. First of all, there are no words written on the cave walls. You saw them briefly, then they vanished. That's your brain at work, not a ghost."

"I saw them on my *camera*," I said loudly. "I had proof before I dropped it. Maybe . . . maybe Ana messed with my camera, like Levi did."

"Levi didn't alter photos, he sent you messages." Roland opened the cooler and pulled out a tangerine. "But for the sake of argument, let's say you're right, and Ana somehow added those words just in the photos. *I want out*, because she wants to get away from the media attention. But based on the story you told, Ana wasn't the one who hated the media. Flavia was."

I opened my mouth to argue, then closed it.

"Flavia was the one who got angry with reporters harassing her daughter. Flavia was the one who became a recluse. Flavia was the one who kept Ana's illness a secret." Roland eyed me as he peeled his tangerine. "I don't recall you or Oscar ever mentioning how Ana felt about it. And I think it's very telling that you interpreted *I want out* to mean *Ana's* desire to get away from unwanted attention, all things considered."

My face grew warm. "What do you mean?"

"Because that's what *you* want." He popped a slice into his mouth. "It's pretty obvious you hate the cameras, Kat."

"So . . . wait." I sat up straighter, my palms suddenly sweaty. "You think I'm making this up?"

Roland shook his head. "No. I think your mind is tricking you into seeing things that aren't really there."

"So you *do* think I'm nuts," I said, stung. "Look, I wasn't faking that Ouija message. And I had pictures of the words in the cave *and* of that ghost."

"Right—that ghost you convinced yourself was a girl," Roland said. "Just like you convinced yourself Ana hated media attention, despite never having actually read that about her. When I say you only thought you saw Ana, I don't mean you're making this up on purpose. I think your brain is occupied with your own situation, and it projected your issues onto the idea of Ana. It tricked you into imagining her."

"Like you imagined Ellie?" Sam said with a smirk.

Roland dropped his tangerine. I tried to hand it back to him, but he was gazing at Sam, mouth slightly open. I'd never seen Roland actually, genuinely speechless before. It was pretty funny, but also kind of unnerving.

"Who's Ellie?" I asked. Roland didn't respond. He and Sam just stared at each other, and I had the weird sense that some sort of silent conversation was going on that I couldn't hear. "Hel-*lo*?" I said, louder. "Who's Ellie?"

"Kat, check it out!"

I tore my eyes off Roland's still-shocked expression to see Mi Jin hurrying toward us, waving my Elapse. All thoughts of the mysterious Ellie momentarily flew from my mind.

"Is it working?" I asked eagerly, hopping off the rock.

Mi Jin beamed. "Yes! I mean, it turns on, at least." She handed it to me, and I flipped the power button on immediately. A message began blinking on the screen:

No memory card in slot.

"It's right here," Mi Jin said, showing me the card. "But it's useless. I had to take it out to get the camera to work. Sorry you lost those photos."

"That's okay," I said, even though it wasn't. Now I had no way to prove to Roland that I wasn't imagining any of that stuff last night. I glanced over at him, expecting a smug comment. But he was staring blankly at the waterfall, completely oblivious to the rest of us.

CHAPTER SIX
DON'T SIT TOO CLOSE TO THE SCREEN

From: EdieM@mymail.net
To: acciopancakes@mymail.net

Hi, KitKat,

Stage fright, hmm? Don't worry, it's completely normal to feel a little awkward on camera. Did I ever tell you about my first day shooting *The Monster in Her Closet*? I didn't think I was nervous at all when I got to the set. Sat down at the kitchen table with my movie parents. Director yelled, "Action." Opened my mouth, and . . . puked Cheerios all over the tablecloth. I still live in fear that they'll release those outtakes one day.

My advice: Practice! Don't roll your eyes at me, young lady. That snazzy camera I got you takes video, right? Lock yourself in a room, turn it on, and record yourself. Dance, recite a poem, sing "All the Single Ladies"—whatever you want. No one's going to see it; this is just for you to get used to being YOU on camera.

Have you and your dad found out any more about the show's schedule over the next few months? Lots of wedding planning going on here, and your mom really wants you to be a part of as much as possible!

Love you,

Grandma

AS far as I could tell, Sam and Roland kept their word and didn't tell anyone my Ana Arias theory. Roland didn't even tease me about it, although I suspected that had less to do with believing me, and more to do with Sam bringing up Ellie, whoever she was. Either way, I was determined to prove Roland wrong. It was just stage fright. And stage fright didn't include hallucinating ghosts and messages on cave walls. Ana had followed me, and I wanted to figure out why.

I felt guilty for not telling Oscar. Back in Rotterdam, I'd confided in him about seeing Sonja Hillebrandt's ghost, and he and I didn't even like each other then. But I still just didn't trust him not to go straight to Jess to try to get us even more screen time.

What made me feel even worse was that this whole Ana thing probably *would* be good for the show. Emily might have been the reason the last episode got so much publicity, but viewers were interested in the Red Leer part, too. If another ghost was "haunting" the show, the fans would eat it up. That's why I kept telling myself that as soon as I got my stupid stage fright under control, I would go to Jess and tell her everything.

In the meantime, Oscar was spending more and more time on the *P2P* message boards. He gave me constant updates about anything and everything that the fans said about either of us, despite me repeatedly telling him I didn't care. If there were any rude comments about me, Oscar didn't mention them, and I resisted the urge to look. Because when I checked my last post the night we got back from camping,

I'd found another comment from the same troll.

kbold04: deleting my comment doesnt change the fact that ur UGLLYYYYYYY

I deleted it, of course. But not before taking a screenshot. Then I'd gone to my blog settings and changed it so that no comments would be published until I approved them. It would be kind of annoying to keep up with, but better than everybody seeing everything this person said about me.

On our last night in Salvador, Dad and the rest of the crew went out for a celebratory dinner after three intense days of editing the waterfall episode. Oscar and I had opted for celebratory pizza and ice pops at the hotel after three intense days of cramming in schoolwork.

"How much do you think we'll actually be in the episode?" Oscar asked, grabbing another maracujá ice pop from the freezer. I made a face.

"Hopefully not much." I'd secretly been hoping Jess would edit us out completely, but no such luck. Yesterday she'd even stopped by after lunch just to tell me and Oscar how great we were. Even Roland seemed pleased with how the episode was turning out.

Oscar ignored my comment. "I hope they use the part where Roland and I found that cold spot. I don't think you were there for that—you went off with Brenda."

"Yeah." I tossed my ice pop stick in the trash can next to the bed. "Did I tell you I checked out that cave behind the waterfall?" I said it as casually as possible, even though the memory caused the hairs on the back of my neck to stand up. *I WANT OUT.* I wanted to tell Oscar about it. I had to. Maybe he was all caught up in this TV stuff, but he was still my friend. I could trust him.

"Really?" He sat up. "Oh man, we should've tried the Ouija board there."

I blinked. "What?"

"In the cave." Oscar pointed his ice pop at my camera sitting on the desk. "We could've shot another video."

"Why would we do that?" I said, trying not to sound too irritated. "The Flavia video was just so Jess could see if we'd be okay on the show."

"Yeah, but think about it." Oscar leaned forward eagerly. "Everyone loved it, even Fright TV. We could make it like a web series! A new video before every episode."

"No, thanks."

"Why not?"

"My blog's enough work already," I said shortly. "Not interested."

Oscar sighed. "Look, if it's that you're afraid of being on camera, I'll do that part and you can just do the research."

"I'm not afraid," I snapped, standing up and grabbing my camera. "For your information, that research takes a lot of time. Besides, you're already going to be on TV. Do you really need a web series, too?"

Oscar rolled his eyes. "It's not about me, Kat. This would

be good for the show. But if you don't want to do it, fine."

"I don't want to do it."

"Fine." He opened his laptop without another word. I left him glued to the fan forums and stalked back to my room, fuming the whole way. *Afraid of being on camera.* That had stung, because it was true. Apparently everyone could tell. If I was going to get over my stage fright, I'd have to take Grandma's advice.

"Okay." Carefully, I set my Elapse on top of the TV so it was about eye level, and flipped it on. Taking a few steps back, I attempted to smile at it. But my skin was already starting to crawl, and my stomach squirmed unpleasantly.

"No one's going to see this," I told the camera. "*Ever.* This is just for practice. You're going to burn this memory card. You're going to break it in half and throw it into the ocean. You're going to put it in a blender then flush it down the toilet. No one will ever see this, no one will ever watch you talking to yourself, so just. Freaking. Relax."

But it wasn't working. If anything, my anxiety doubled. Scowling, I reached out and flipped the camera off. Almost immediately, my pulse began to slow. I took the Elapse and sat on the edge of the bed to watch the video.

"No one's going to see this. Ever."

Once again, I found myself scrutinizing my appearance. My hair was pulled back in its usual super-short ponytail. I wondered what sort of "stylish" cut my mom envisioned. I wondered what she'd say about my *Creature from the Black*

Lagoon shirt (probably "Do you *have* to wear that to the dinner table?"). I wondered what she'd say about my blotchy, bug-bite-covered skin and the sunburn that was the result of all the hiking and afternoons on the beach. I wondered...

... why there was someone in the mirror on the video.

I shot to my feet, turning to glance at the mirror before hitting replay. This time, I ignored myself and stared hard at the mirror behind me. For a few seconds, all I saw was the reflection of the Elapse on top of the TV. I squinted harder as the clip came to an end.

"Just. Freaking. Relax."

There. Right when video-me said, "Relax," there was movement—something, someone, passing between me and the TV in a lightning-fast blur. Goose bumps broke out all over my arms, and I spent at least a full minute staring at the real mirror before watching the video again. And again. And again.

My heart was pounding out of control, so I turned the camera off and set it down. I paced around the room, rubbing my arms and glancing at the mirror every few seconds.

I couldn't prove it was Ana. But it was clearly *something.* I had proof I wasn't seeing things.

The problem was, proving it meant showing people this video. This video of me giving myself a pep talk about my stupid stage fright. Which happened to be the exact reason my brain was tricking me into seeing Ana's ghost, according to Roland. What if—a shiver passed through me at the thought—what if Jess wanted me to put this video on my blog? What if she wanted to *use it in an episode*?

"Nope," I said loudly and decisively, grabbing the Elapse again. I pulled the memory card out and tucked it securely in my pocket just as the door flew open.

"Look at this!" Oscar hurried in carrying his laptop, which he shoved in my face. Startled, I dropped my camera onto the bed and took the laptop with both hands.

To: acciopancakes@mymail.net, oscarisnotagrouch@mymail.net
From: ShellyMathers@Rumorz.net
Subject: Interview on Rumorz!

Hi, Kat and Oscar!
I'm a writer on staff at *Rumorz*, a website that covers all the latest in entertainment news and reviews. I've been covering many of Fright TV's shows for years, including *Passport to Paranormal*—you may have seen my article on the incident at Daems Penitentiary a few weeks ago.

Thomas Cooper, Fright TV's Executive VP, mentioned that you two are about to become cast members yourselves. How exciting! I was wondering if you'd be interested in doing an interview for *Rumorz*? I'd love to hear more about your blog, Kat, and any other juicy "behind the scenes" tidbits you'd like to share! Let me know if we can set up a call, preferably sometime before your next episode airs.
Thanks a bunch!
Shelly Mathers

"Oh yes, please, I'd love to do an interview with a trashy gossip website," I said sarcastically. "We'll give them all the juicy stuff, like how Jess bleaches her hair or that Roland wears Batman pajamas."

"Come on, Kat!" Oscar took his laptop back, scanning the e-mail again. "We should totally do this. No cameras or anything, and she said she'd call. It'd be great publicity for the show *and* your blog."

"That's the thing," I said. "I already say all the behind-the-scenes stuff I want to say on my blog. I don't have anything else to talk about. And my grandma always says *Rumorz* is really sleazy," I added. "This reporter probably thinks she can trick us into giving her some real dirt."

Oscar made a face. "Still . . . it'd be cool to do an interview. It's like we're actually celebrities."

I fought the urge to roll my eyes. "Look, you can do it if you want. But you should probably at least ask Lidia first."

"Mmm," Oscar said noncommittally. By the look on his face, I could tell he was already giving an interview in his head. Probably on the red carpet.

Our seven-hour flight to Argentina turned into a twenty-seven-hour flight thanks to a monsoon. Well, not an *official* monsoon. But the sheets of rain slamming into the windows at the São Paulo airport all night during our extended layover was the loudest storm I'd ever heard—loud enough to keep us from sleeping. (The hard plastic seats didn't help much, either.) By the time our plane touched down in Buenos Aires, the entire *Passport to Paranormal* cast looked more like *Night of the Living Dead*.

"It's a few minutes after seven," Lidia croaked, heaving her suitcase into the back of our rental van. "If we luck out with traffic, we might make it to the hotel before nine."

"And so far, we've had tons of travel luck," muttered Roland, unwrapping what had to be the hundredth sucker he'd had since we left Salvador.

No one spoke much in the van. I kept nodding off, my head dropping onto my chest before I jerked awake. The next thing I knew, the van pulled to an abrupt halt in front of the hotel. I sat up, startled, and realized I'd slept on Oscar's shoulder the whole way there. Which maybe would've been embarrassing, but he was literally drooling on the window, so I figured he hadn't noticed.

"We're here," I said, poking him in the arm.

"But I can't play the piano," he mumbled, and I giggled despite my exhaustion.

"*Oscar.* Wake up."

He blinked blearily at me, then squinted out the window. "Hotel?"

"Yup."

"Bed. Need bed." Oscar staggered out of the van, yawning. Lidia tossed him his duffel bag, which he caught with a grunt.

"You can turn in if you want, but I kind of thought you'd like to watch yourself on TV first," she said teasingly. At that, Oscar's eyes flew open.

"Nope, I'm awake!"

I smiled, but my heart fluttered against my rib cage. In the haze of delayed flights and neck-cramp-inducing naps at the airport, I'd managed to put the fact that tonight was the night I would make my television debut mostly out of my mind.

By nine o'clock, all eight of us were crammed into Lidia and Oscar's room. The warm scent of coffee filled the air, and the adults all looked much perkier. I was, too, although my adrenaline had more to do with fear than caffeine.

Mi Jin crouched by the TV with her laptop, face scrunched in concentration as she tried connecting them with different combinations of cables, cords, and adapters. I could see Fright TV's website on the laptop screen; all episodes were available to stream at the same time as they aired on television back in the US.

"Got it!" Mi Jin said triumphantly, and everyone cheered as the network's site appeared on the TV. I faked a cheer, too, shrinking back into my pillow. As if he'd read my mind, Dad slung his arm around my shoulders.

"Don't worry," he said as the opening credits started. "I watched this about a thousand times while we were editing. You and Oscar did great, so just relax!"

I tried to smile, thinking of the memory card in my pocket and the secret it held. *Just. Freaking. Relax.* Hoping no one else could tell how nervous I was, I leaned into Dad and squeezed my balled-up fists in my lap.

But it turned out Dad was right. The first time I saw myself on TV, I winced a little. After a few minutes, though, I was used to it. Sort of.

Oscar was way better at this than me; that much was screamingly obvious. Everything I said was clipped, and sometimes I mumbled. I also turned away from the cameras a lot. But Oscar spoke clearly and was pretty much the opposite of camera shy. If anything, he came off as a little too eager, at least in my opinion.

My favorite part was near the beginning, when we were setting up camp. Mi Jin must have sneaked up to the ledge, because she'd recorded me and Oscar joking around about Elsa battling the Abominable Snowman, right before I jumped into the pool. Neither of us knew she was there, so we both sounded like ourselves.

All of the non-me parts of the episode were great. Sam had been in top form, picking up all sorts of emotions from the residual haunting, piecing together a story of what he thought happened to the campers. Dad added to that with facts he'd learned about them—their families, where they went to school, their interests—which made Sam's increasingly intense descriptions of their fear and panic as they realized they were going to die even more sympathetic and horrifying. And just when things would get really heavy, Roland would lighten the mood with a quip. Until the last few minutes.

In a voiceover, Dad talked about why the waterfall was

likely the perfect example of a residual haunting, while clips of our hike back to the van played. But at one point when we stopped to rest, Jess took her camera over to Roland and Sam, who were sitting on the rail of a rusty train track, passing a water bottle back and forth. Roland's expression was distant, and I suddenly remembered that this had been filmed just a few hours after the whole Ellie conversation.

"So, what's the verdict, guys?" Jess asked. "Skeptics argue that the reason anyone feels anxiety or fear at the site of a supposed residual haunting, the reason they think they hear or even see the event replaying, is simply because of the story itself—the same reason people think they hear noises in the attic or check under their beds after watching a scary movie, even though they know it's fiction. Can we ever prove this kind of phenomenon is real?"

Sam opened his mouth to respond, but Roland beat him to it.

"It doesn't matter." His voice had none of its usual sarcasm. "Proof doesn't matter. What matters is whether you believe or not. Maybe . . . maybe sometimes belief is enough to make it real."

With that, he handed the bottle to Sam, whose eyes were so comically round with surprise that everyone in the room started sniggering.

"You out Sam'd Sam," Mi Jin told Roland between giggles, and he grinned. But I couldn't help noticing that his eyes looked sad.

"My granddaughter, the television star!"

I snorted, cradling the phone with my shoulder and scrolling through the newer comments on my last blog post. "I don't think *star* is the right word."

"You were *fantastic*," Grandma said for, like, the hundredth time. "If you hadn't sent me that e-mail about being nervous in front of the cameras, I never would've known. Did you try practicing alone?"

"Er . . ." I touched my pocket self-consciously. "Yeah, once."

"And it helped?"

Yes, but not with my stage fright. "A little," I replied. "I feel pretty dumb talking to myself, though."

"You should recite something," Grandma suggested. "Just pick a movie and start quoting it. My monologue near the end of *Return to the Asylum* is particularly good. Or . . . what's that now?" Her voice got muffled, and I could hear someone talking in the background. "Oh, of course . . . Kat?"

"Yeah?"

"I'm going to pass the phone over to your mom, okay?" Grandma sounded way too chipper all of a sudden. "It's getting late, and she has to head home soon."

I clicked over to my inbox, realizing I still needed to respond to Trish. My heart leaped when I saw a new e-mail from Jamie. "Sure." As Grandma handed Mom the phone, I opened Jamie's message.

To: acciopancakes@mymail.net
From: jamiebaggins@mymail.net
Subject: ALL CAPS WARNING

THAT EPISODE WAS AMAZING AND YOU ARE EVEN
MORE AMAZING AND HEY GUESS WHAT I'LL SEE YOU
TOMORROW!!

I was grinning like a dork when Mom got on the phone.

"Hi, Kat."

"Hey." I decided to respond to Jamie entirely in emojis. *Sun. Beach. Sandals. Ghost. Skull.*

"How cool was that?" Mom said in a fake-perky voice I knew all too well. "My daughter, on TV. Looks like you're having fun!"

"Yup, Dad and I are having a great time." *Pizza. Devil. Thumbs-up.*

Mom was quiet for a few seconds. "So the next episode is in a haunted . . . church?"

"Yeah." *Church. Ghost. Skull. Ghost. Skull.* "There are catacombs under it. Lots of bones, and the ghost of a nun, supposedly."

"Wow. When do you start filming?"

Palm tree. Popsicle. Spider. "In a few days, I guess," I said. "This investigation is a little different. There's a psychology professor from a university in Buenos Aires that's been holding séances down there as part of a big research project with his students. They say they've actually contacted this nun, like, a bunch of times. So I think Dad's going to spend

88

some time interviewing him, plus he's got to research the history of the catacombs and all that."

"Ah."

I felt a little stab of vindictive pleasure. Mom couldn't have cared less about the show or dead nuns or any of this, and I definitely didn't need to talk about Dad so much. But sometimes the only way I could get through these conversations was by playing a game. I called it: *How long can I keep Mom from talking about herself?*

"So . . . I finally decided on the bridesmaid dresses!"

I almost laughed out loud. That didn't last long. "Yeah?" *Bathing suit. Ice cream. Bloody footsteps.*

"I'm e-mailing you a link right now, okay?"

"Sure." I sighed, scanning my ridiculous response to Jamie. I needed one more emoji.

Heart.

I blushed and tapped *Delete*. Too soon.

Heart eyes.

After clicking *Send*, I went back to my inbox and found Mom's e-mail. I groaned inwardly when I saw the link—not to a dress shop, but to one of her Facebook albums. Haunted prisons and catacombs were no big deal, but I rarely ventured into the fearsome place that was my mother's Facebook page. It never used to be that bad—mostly just photos she'd taken, which were always great, considering she's a professional. But ever since she left me and Dad, it was like she turned into a teenager again. Not that there's anything *wrong* with adults saying things like "squee!" and taking tons of selfies, but it's just weird when it's your parent. One time she commented "YOLO" on her own status update, and I wanted to set my computer on fire.

This album was called "Wedding Prep!" and the first photo was of Mom's maid of honor, Kathleen. The dress was pale purple with spaghetti straps and a flouncy skirt that ended at the knee.

"Nice."

"You like it?" Mom asked eagerly.

"I guess." I paused, taking a deep breath. If I was going to do it, now was the time. *Mom . . . I don't want to be a bridesmaid in your wedding.*

"We'll have to set up a fitting as soon as you know when you'll be back," Mom went on in a rush. "I've got one scheduled next week for me and Elena. You should see her, Kat," she added, and the fondness in her voice made my stomach drop. "She refuses to take her flower-girl dress off; it's the sweetest thing. She even tries to sleep in it!"

I forced a laugh. "That's cute. Anyway, um . . . I'm not sure when Dad and I will be back next. Thomas Cooper from Fright TV is coming in tomorrow, and they're supposed to go over scheduling through this summer. And . . ."

"Don't worry, your father and I will work it out," Mom cut in. "Honey, I've got to run. Talk to you soon, okay?"

"Okay."

"Love you."

"Bye," I mumbled. It wasn't until after I hung up that something dawned on me.

Mom had just watched me on television, and she hadn't done her usual compliment-that's-really-criticism-in-disguise thing. Nothing about how cute my hair would look if I curled it. No saying, "Have you tried this lotion? It has sunscreen *and* it evens out your skin tone!" No recommending mascara, eye shadow, or anything that "doesn't even look like you're wearing makeup at all!" (Then what's the point of wearing it in the first place, Mom?)

For a few seconds, I actually thought maybe this was improvement. Maybe Grandma had talked to her or something. Then, just as I was about to close her Facebook album, my eyes fell on a photo. Mom was standing next to her car with a few giant shopping bags hanging on one arm. Elena clung to her other arm, holding out the skirt of what I assumed was her flower-girl dress—the same pale purple as Kathleen's dress, but with ten times the poofiness. She and Mom were both beaming. The caption under the photo said, *Look at my little princess!*

I closed the tab quickly, feeling stupid. Of course Mom hadn't stopped criticizing me because she thought I was okay the way I was. She didn't care if I liked that stuff anymore because now she had a daughter who did.

Rumorz
All the celebrity gossip you need (and then some)!

Interview with New *P2P* Cast Member Oscar Bettencourt by Shelly Mathers

Happy Friday, *Rumorz* readers! It's another frigid December day here in New York, and I don't know about you, but I could really use a little sun, sand, and . . . ghosts?

Many of you Fright TV fanatics already tune in to *Passport to Paranormal*—and if you didn't before last month's exciting episode in Brussels that culminated in the arrest of Emily Rosinski, I bet you do now! Wednesday's episode, filmed in the wild jungles of Brazil, may not have had a crazy former-host-turned-stalker, but it did feature two new cast members . . . and they're only thirteen years old! I caught up with Oscar Bettencourt on the phone while he and the rest of the *P2P* crew waited out a thunderstorm in the São Paulo airport. We had just enough time for a quick Q&A before he took off for sunny Argentina.

S: Thanks for taking the time to chat with me, Oscar! Most kids your age are stuck at a school desk, but you're traveling around the world hunting ghosts! How'd you manage that?

O: My aunt is the producer on *P2P*. I grew up in Portland with my other aunt, but last summer Aunt Lidia asked if I wanted to start traveling with her and the show starting in the fall.

S: Wow! And you were okay with leaving your home, your

school—all your friends—behind?

O: Yes. Definitely.

S: So you were at Daems Penitentiary with the crew a few weeks ago, but you weren't a cast member yet. Why do you think Fright TV decided to add you to the show?

O: Because of my charm and good looks? Just kidding. I think it's because of Kat's blog. It started getting really popular with some of the fans, and the network noticed.

S: I've read her blog! Very interesting stuff. I especially loved that video of the two of you, the one with the Ouija board . . . so fun to get extra content like that! Can we look forward to any more of those?

O: Yeah, definitely! In fact, I have some news about that.

S: Ooh, an exclusive! Do tell!

O: Starting next week, I'll be hosting a web series on Kat's blog called the *Graveyard Slot.* Every Sunday at midnight, we'll post a new video with even more behind-the-scenes footage!

S: How exciting! So we can expect one this Sunday?

O: Yup! There'll be one for each episode. Maybe even more. We're heading to China for the next episode, but I think we'll be in New York for a few days before that . . . seems like a good place for a bonus video!

S: Fantastic! You and Kat have been such a great addition to the show. Although I have to tell you, not everyone seems to be on board. I don't know if you saw Rick Wallace's recent review of the Brazil episode over on *Mixed Bag,* but he thinks this is just Fright TV's desperate attempt to draw in a younger audience, and it'll alienate the adult viewers they already have. To quote Rick: "If I wanted a scary tween experience, I'd just talk to my daughter and her friends about whatever boy band they're currently obsessed with. Stop dumbing down your shows just for ratings, Fright TV."

O: Ooookay . . . Well, I didn't see that review, but some of the other cast members were worried about that, too, so I'm not surprised.

S: Really? Like who?

93

O: Um . . . it doesn't matter, because after the last episode, I don't think they're worried anymore. And it's kind of funny that Rick Whatshisname takes ghosts seriously, but not kids. If an adult is embarrassed about being into something kids are into, that's their problem. Besides, just because a show—or a band, or whatever—is popular with kids, that doesn't automatically mean it's dumb.

S: Ha! Great point. Maybe Rick should give his daughter's music a shot, too.

O: He should. Oh, I think my flight's about to start boarding.

S: Aw, too bad. Maybe we can schedule a longer interview later? I'm sure our *Rumorz* readers have tons more questions for you!

O: Definitely!

S: Great! Thanks again, Oscar! Looking forward to seeing more of you and Kat on *P2P*.

'D been sitting on the sofa in the hotel lobby for over an hour, running down the battery on my phone. Jamie and Hailey were supposed to arrive any minute, and I was just a little bit excited to see them. But the new comments on my last blog post were doing a nice job of distracting me, because there were over twenty of them. Each and every one from kbold04. The first one said:

> **kbold04:** i know u wont publish my comments but that doesnt mean u wont read them so let me tell u sumthings

The comments that followed were . . . mean. *Really* mean. Vile, even.

For some reason, I couldn't stop reading them. After a few minutes, without allowing myself to think too hard about why I was doing it, I'd taken a screenshot of every single comment before deleting them from my blog. Then I'd spent the next hour going over the screenshots one by one, letting each ugly word burn into my brain.

The elevator doors slid open, and Dad and Jess stepped out. I stuffed my phone in my pocket, hands shaking. If Dad saw those comments, he would totally lose it.

"Wild jungles of Brazil?" Dad was saying, staring down at Jess's phone. "Well, that's inaccurate. Not to mention ignorant."

Jess gave a humorless laugh. "Keep reading."

"Hey, Dad," I called, hoping I sounded normal. "Have you seen Oscar? He's supposed to meet me down here."

Dad and Jess exchanged a glance. "Yeah, he's upstairs talking with Lidia. He might be a little late."

I frowned. "Is everything okay?"

"He's fine. Kat, did you know about this interview?"

"What interview?"

Before Dad could respond, someone squealed behind me. "Kat!"

I spun around as Hailey Cooper came barreling through the doors, curly brown ponytail flying behind her. Grinning, I braced myself as she tackle-hugged me, squeezing my ribs so hard I could barely breathe. "Hi!" I managed to squeak.

"I saw you on TV!" Hailey cried, bouncing up and down on her toes. "Mom actually let me have a viewing party on a school night! A bunch of my friends came—it was seriously, like, half the sixth grade at my school, and some seventh-

and eighth-graders, too. Even Natalie Blackwell came, which was just, oh my God—anyway, most of them had never seen a single episode of *P2P* but they *totally* loved it and—"

I tried to keep up with Hailey's excited chatter while glancing at the entrance every other second. When Jamie finally came in, dragging two suitcases, I felt a huge smile stretch my cheeks.

"Hey, Kat!" he exclaimed, hauling both bags over. "Forget something, Hailey?"

"Oh yeah," Hailey said sheepishly as she took her suitcase from her brother. Jamie hesitated, then gave me a quick hug. I pictured my last e-mail to him and suddenly felt embarrassed about the heart eyes. Flirting online was a lot easier than it was in real life.

I helped Jamie and Hailey move their luggage over to the couches. Soon Dad and Jess were busy talking to Thomas Cooper, who looked just as stuffy and disinterested in everyone and everything around him as ever. Meanwhile, Hailey filled me in on what she thought of Oscar and me being cast members ("*SO JEALOUS*"), what she thought of the waterfall episode ("*loved it, except what was the deal with Roland being all weird at the end?*"), and what her friends from school thought ("*most of them loved it, too, although a few said ghost hunting wasn't their 'thing,' which is their loss, obviously*"). When she finally paused for breath, Jamie jumped in so skillfully, I had to stifle a laugh.

"So where's Oscar?"

"Up in his room," I said, glancing at the elevator. "He was going to meet me down here, but Dad said Lidia needed to talk to him. Want to see if they're done?"

"Sure!"

After Jamie got their room key from Mr. Cooper, who was now deep in conversation with Dad and Jess, the three of us headed up to drop off their suitcases. Lidia passed us in the hall, and—after returning Hailey's bone-crunching hug—turned and called: "Oscar, the Coopers are here! We were just on the way down," she added, ruffling Hailey's hair fondly. "Is Jess with your dad already?"

"Yup! They're still in the lobby." Hailey peered around Lidia, her eyes widening. *"Oscaaaar!"* she bellowed, taking off down the corridor with her arms outspread. Oscar, who had just stepped out of his room, put his arms up like a shield and staggered back inside with a look of mock terror. Hailey followed, and a moment later there was a shriek and a series of thumps that sounded like bowling balls being dropped onto the floor, followed by a very emphatic expletive Oscar probably wouldn't have said if he'd known his aunt could hear him, along with Hailey's wild laughter. Lidia gazed at the door to her room for a few seconds, then turned to me.

"I don't want to know what that was," she said decisively. "And I'd like it to be cleaned up before I can find out."

I grinned. "No problem."

Lidia headed to the elevators while Jamie and I ventured

into her room to find Hailey in hysterics on the bathroom floor. Oscar stood in the tub, wearing a bemused expression. He was aiming the removable showerhead at Hailey as if he'd meant to use it as weapon, but instead the water was gushing straight from the pipe and drenching him head to toe. The rack that hung from the showerhead had tilted when Oscar yanked it out, causing the bottles it held to fall and spilling soapy goo all over the tub and floor. Bubbles were quickly rising around his legs.

"Most people take their clothes off before they shower," I told him, which just made Hailey laugh even harder. Oscar responded by whipping a soaking-wet loofah at my face.

It was a few minutes before we managed to pull ourselves together and clean up the mess. After drying off and changing his clothes, Oscar joined the rest of us in his room.

"We were just telling Kat about the viewing party we had for your first episode," Jamie told him.

Oscar's face brightened. "Viewing party?"

Jamie nodded. "A bunch of people from school came over. I think some of them might even start watching regularly now!"

"Well, Natalie Blackwell definitely will," Hailey added knowingly. "She has a *massive* crush on you." She gave Oscar a look that seemed to mean he was supposed to be flattered or impressed. Probably both.

His brow furrowed. "Who?"

"Natalie. *Blackwell*." Hailey stared at him, her blue eyes

wide. "She's *so cool*. Her family owns the Blackwell Building, which is super haunted. She's practically famous. I told her I could set you guys up when you come to New York. Like on a *date*."

"It's a big deal, Oscar," Jamie added solemnly. "First, Natalie Blackwell. Next thing you know, you're dating Taylor Swift."

Hailey glowered at us, arms crossed, as we started snickering uncontrollably. "It *is* a big deal, but whatever."

Before she could pick up her breathless ramble again, I turned to Oscar. "Hey, why didn't you come down earlier?"

"Oh!" Oscar leaned across me to grab his iPad off the table. "Aunt Lidia was chewing me out about something." He swiped the screen a few times, pressing his lips together like he was trying not to smile.

"You seem pretty happy about getting yelled at," Jamie observed, and now Oscar was grinning for real.

"Because it was worth it. Check it out!"

He turned the iPad around so we could see the screen, and I groaned.

"Oh my *God*. You actually did that *Rumorz* interview?"

"Whoa, awesome!" Hailey exclaimed, and she and Jamie started to read. I gave Oscar a look.

"You didn't ask Lidia first, did you?"

He wrinkled his nose. "I was going to, seriously. I e-mailed Shelly back, but I figured I'd have time to ask Aunt Lidia about actually doing the interview on the flight. But Shelly responded really fast and asked me to call while we were stuck at the airport, and I . . . well, I did." He smiled nonchalantly, but I saw a flash of guilt in his eyes before I leaned in to read.

"If an adult is embarrassed about being into something kids are into, that's their problem," Hailey murmured under her breath. "Seriously, though."

Jamie started laughing. "Wow, I can see why Lidia might be upset," he said when he finished reading. "Rick Wallace is kind of a big deal as far as critics go—I've heard Dad griping about him before. And you just straight-up insulted him on a rival website. Which is awesome, by the way," he added, and Oscar beamed.

"Thanks."

"That was *great*," Hailey said fervently, pushing the iPad closer to me. "I didn't know you guys were starting a web series! *Graveyard Slot*, that's so cool!"

I bit my lip hard, still staring at the screen even though I'd finished reading. My good mood was quickly vanishing, replaced by anger. Still, I tried to keep my voice light as I looked up at Oscar.

"Yeah, I didn't know that, either! When did we decide that?"

He met my gaze steadily. "Well, Jess and I talked about it, and she—"

"You suggested it to Jess?" My voice wasn't so light anymore, but I didn't care. "Even though . . ." I stopped myself before saying the rest. *Even though I didn't want to.*

I didn't want Jamie and Hailey to know I'd rejected Oscar's idea because of my stupid camera aversion.

"Look," Oscar said quickly. "Jess mentioned the network liked the first video, and all I said was it'd be a cool regular feature, and then she said she'd talk to you about it."

"Which she hasn't." I pointed at his screen. "And yet?"

"Right." Oscar was starting to look more exasperated than guilty. "Okay, I guess I shouldn't have mentioned it to Shelly without talking to you. But this will be good promotion for the show, and I'll do all the on-camera stuff, and . . . and Jamie and Hailey can help with the research! Do you guys want to maybe be in the next one?" he asked them, turning away from the evil eye I was giving him.

Hailey gasped. "Are you kidding me?" She grabbed her brother's arm and shook it frantically. "Do you think Dad would let us? We could convince him, right?"

"Um . . . possibly. If Kat wants." Jamie looked at me for an answer, but I was still too busy glaring at Oscar. He was doing his best to look contrite, but I could tell he was equally annoyed with me. If the Coopers weren't sitting right there, I knew exactly what he'd say.

Get over it already.

"Can we, Kat? Please, please, please?" Hailey begged, bouncing up and down on the bed. I tried to smile at her, but inside I was seething. I didn't *want* to do a web series. But now Hailey was all excited about the idea of being a part of the show.

Jamie, however, obviously knew something was up. "It's a lot of extra work for Kat," he told his sister. "She already writes all those posts, and it takes a lot of time—"

"But we can help, like Oscar said!" Hailey cried. "I'll find a place to hold a séance and do all the research, I swear! Oh come on, it'll be so much fun!" She clasped her hands together, giving me her best puppy-dog eyes. Exhaling, I smiled at her.

"Yeah, let's do it."

"*Yes!*" Hailey pumped her fist in the air, then snatched Oscar's iPad out of his hands. "Okay, I'm gonna start looking up places right now." As she began swiping away, I got up and headed over to the laptop set up at the desk. I was too angry to look at Oscar. Seriously, what was the deal with his weird new attention-seeking thing? He was obsessed with reading about himself on the *P2P* forums. All it took was this *Rumorz* reporter telling him she'd love to see more videos of him, and he'd gone and committed *me* to doing a web series on *my* blog. He'd obviously planned this out before his interview—he'd even come up with a name for the series, the *Graveyard Slot*. He must have known I'd be furious, but he just did it anyway. For what? More fan comments gushing about how cute and funny he was? Ugh.

"Are you sure this is okay?" Jamie asked quietly, startling me. He'd moved over to sit on the edge of the bed right behind me. I turned in my chair.

"Yeah, it's fine. Just caught me off guard."

"Okay." He smiled at me, and as always, I couldn't help but smile back. Part of me wanted to tell him the real reason I was so upset. That a web series just meant more camera time, which meant more nausea and stress. And, undoubtedly, more horrible comments from kbold04.

But I wasn't sure he'd understand, because nothing ever seemed to bother Jamie. His parents were often too busy to spend any real time with him and his sister, but Jamie just shrugged it off and got on with stuff. It did seem like the smart thing to do. Self-absorbed mom wants you to be in her wedding even though the idea clearly makes you miserable? Who cares! Being on television makes you want to jump out of your own skin and hide under your bed forever? Whatever! Get over it.

I wanted to get over it. *All* of it. But it just wasn't that easy for me.

CHAPTER EIGHT
... BUT WORDS CAN ALWAYS HURT ME

Post: Brunilda Cano, el fantasma de la Catedral de Nuestra Señora de la Encarnación
Comments: (168)

Over the next few days, we're going to be filming in the Cathedral of Our Lady of the Incarnation in Nueva Pompeya, a neighborhood in south Buenos Aires. The church, built in 1756, isn't anywhere near the largest one in the city, but it does have something that makes it pretty unique: catacombs. Yesterday, we took a tour of the underground tombs. I don't want to spoil too much of the episode, but:

1) the walls are made from thousands of human bones and skulls, and

2) yes, it was hands down the coolest and creepiest thing I've ever seen.

Of course, plenty of people believe the catacombs are haunted. Because—HUMAN BONES. But over the last year, someone has actually been trying to prove it. With SCIENCE. Hunting ghosts: It's not just for nutjobs anymore! (If anyone is offended by that, please know I officially consider myself a nutjob.)

Professor Emilio Guzmán teaches psychology at the University of Boedo, and he's especially interested in parapsychology. Last year, he started bringing a group of students down to the catacombs once a month to hold a séance and record the results. They've been focusing on one spirit in particular—Brunilda Cano, who was a nun at the cathedral in the nineteenth century. She's an ancestor of Professor Guzmán. AND . . . wait for it . . . she was POSSESSED. He says he has records of an attempted exorcism, but it wasn't successful, and she died November 28, 1891. That's all I've managed to find out so far.

We're meeting Professor Guzmán at the church tomorrow to learn more, but he claims his séances have been really successful. Some of his students have been so frightened by Brunilda's ghost that they've stopped participating entirely. Personally, I can't wait to meet her. Friday night, the whole *P2P* cast is joining Professor Guzmán in the catacombs to contact Brunilda. But Oscar and I don't want to wait that long, which is why we're taking Mi Jin's Ouija board to the church tomorrow. Stay tuned for another episode of our new web series, *Graveyard Slot*, on Sunday at midnight!

THE cathedral was gorgeous: jewel-colored stained glass windows; tall, castle-like towers; pointed arches with intricate carvings; dark gray stone that glittered slightly in the sun; and wicked-looking gargoyles with gaping mouths. "Very Gothic," I observed, much to Dad's delight. (I didn't have the heart to tell him I didn't mean "Gothic Revival" in the architecture sense and more just, well, "goth.")

The inside was just as beautiful, although not as peaceful as it had been when we first visited yesterday, thanks to a large tour group. Most of the *P2P* crew had decided to wait for Professor Guzmán outside, but I was taking pictures of the vaulted ceiling and the images in the stained glass windows (some were impressively gory) while Oscar, Jamie, and Hailey sat in the back pew. They fell silent when the group entered, the tour guide talking loudly in thickly accented English.

I watched them shuffle slowly up the aisle, wondering if it would be rude to take photos of them. Mom always said this was tricky for professional photographers: You didn't want to try and be sneaky about it, but if you asked people if it was okay, you'd never get natural-looking shots because they'd be too aware of the camera. Her rule was to only ask permission if she wanted a close-up of someone's face. Otherwise, she took the pictures she wanted to take and stopped if people seemed uncomfortable.

So I moved to the front near the altar, held my camera up, and waited a few seconds. The tour guide, an older man with salt-and-pepper hair, glanced over his shoulder and smiled at me before turning back to the group.

Click! Click! I got several shots of the whole group, then started focusing on individuals. Two gray-haired women wearing backpacks and sneakers. A girl with dreadlocks and a killer camera that was probably about fifty times more expensive than my Elapse. Two bored-looking girls around Hailey's age, whose parents reacted too enthusiastically to every sentence that came out of the tour guide's mouth. Six or seven people all wearing the same red T-shirts that said *Tapaculo Adventures.* And, in the back, a boy and a girl who weren't paying attention to the guide at all.

I studied them through my viewfinder, zooming in a little. They were both teenagers, and the girl looked like a junior or senior in high school, while the boy was probably a year older than me. Brother and sister, I guessed, seeing as they had the same sun-streaked dark brown hair, brown skin slightly lighter than mine, and noses that bent slightly to the left. No bags or cameras or any touristy stuff, either. They were whispering, heads were bowed together, and the girl kept glancing back at the entrance in a nervous sort of way.

"Hey."

Startled, I lowered my camera to find Oscar at my side. "What?" It came out more clipped than I intended, and he sighed.

"Seriously, you're still mad at me about the *Graveyard Slot* thing? I said I'm sorry."

I stepped aside as the tour group began moving up closer to the altar. "Are you, though?"

Oscar's scowled. "What?"

"Never mind." I didn't feel like getting into it now, especially when Oscar would just deny it. Besides, it seemed wrong to have an argument in a church. But I knew he didn't regret anything. I said no to the web series, but he'd gone and told Jess about it anyway. Then stupid Shelly Mathers had given him the perfect opportunity to seal the deal during their interview. He knew I wouldn't want to disappoint anyone by backing out, and his plan had totally worked.

"Kat . . ."

"Forget it, Oscar. I'm not mad." I zoomed in on Jamie

and Hailey in the last pew, heads bowed over Oscar's iPad, probably still researching places to feature in *Graveyard Slot*. But my hands were really starting to sweat, so after just a few shots, I flipped my camera off and took a deep breath. After a couple of seconds, my heartbeat started to slow.

"Are you getting sick or something?" Oscar asked. "You're really sweaty."

I shook my head, wiping my palms on my shorts. This morning when I'd logged into my blog to approve the new comments, I'd been greeted by another dozen messages from kbold04. He was getting meaner, too. If Dad knew the stuff this person was saying to me, he'd probably flip out and delete my whole blog. So I'd deleted the comments—but not before getting a screenshot of each one. Any time I had a spare second, I pulled out my phone and flipped through them. My stomach had been churning with anxiety all morning, but I couldn't stop reading those horrible things about me.

But I definitely did *not* want to discuss any of that with Mr. TV Celebrity at the moment, and the tour group had stopped at the front of the aisle, within earshot.

"This lovely circular window," the guide was saying as he gestured behind him, "provides a . . . a magnified *focus* for the exterior design, as you will soon see from the courtyard. And there was just as much *focus* on decorative and romantic features on the inside as the outside . . ."

Oscar was watching one of the guys in *Tapaculo*

Adventures shirts closest to us, his eyes narrowed. The guy's shoulders shook with silent laughter every time the guide said *focus*. Probably because with his thick accent, it sounded like "fuh-kyoos." If the guide noticed his reaction— and I was pretty sure he had, since the guy's friend kept punching his arm to get him to stop laughing—he didn't acknowledge it, and kept talking over the snickers.

"Rude," I muttered loud enough for the guy to hear. He glanced over his shoulder at me, pushing his glasses up his nose when they slipped.

"What's that now?"

Before I could respond, Oscar spoke up. "We just want to know what the joke is," he whispered eagerly, leaning closer. A few feet away, the teenage girl was also glaring at Glasses Guy, but her brother was watching Oscar.

Glasses Guy smirked. "Just . . . you know. This dude's kinda hard to understand."

"He is?" Oscar asked, his expression perfectly innocent. "So how do you know what he's saying is so funny?" I had to chew the inside of my cheek to keep myself from smiling, and the teenage girl and her brother looked amused, too. But Glasses Guy didn't seem to pick up on the sarcasm.

"Well, it's more how he says it."

"Ah." Oscar nodded. "Well, I'm sure you speak whatever your second language is perfectly."

Glasses Guy blinked. "I don't speak a . . ." He trailed off, scowling, as he realized even his friend was now laughing at him. "Whatever, kid." They followed the rest of the group as the guide, now talking about the courtyard and the entrance to the catacombs, led them to the exit along the left wall.

Oscar and I headed back to Jamie and Hailey. "Nice," I told him. "That guy was being a jerk."

"Yeah." Oscar smiled a little. "My grandpa had a really thick accent. Drove him nuts when people laughed, even if they weren't making fun of him. And *especially* if they called it 'cute.' So one day he just started calling them out. *Can you say something to me in your second language? Help me understand the correct way to have an accent.* That usually shut them up pretty fast."

The front door creaked open, and Mi Jin waved at us. She held the door as the rest of the crew filed inside, along with a man who I guessed was Professor Guzmán. Jamie and Hailey were already up and moving down the row to join us.

"He's so *tall*," Hailey whispered loudly, and Jamie shushed her. She was right, though—it was hard not to be taken aback by Professor Guzmán's height. He towered above everyone else, and his slightly hunched narrow shoulders, spindly frame, and pointed chin added to the effect. A girl around Mi Jin's age, who I assumed was one of his students, trailed behind him, barely keeping pace with his long strides.

"It's so thrilling to meet a fellow parapsychologist!"

Professor Guzmán was saying to Roland. "I'm sure you know how hard it is to find anyone in the scientific community who doesn't scoff at psychical research. I'm afraid that Brunilda Cano's poor spirit has been the subject of some ridicule since my students and I have reported our successful encounters."

We hurried to keep up with the crew, listening intently as Professor Guzmán talked about Brunilda. He couldn't keep still when he talked, flailing his arms or wiggling his fingers as he described some of his group's most memorable séances.

"Last time, she elevated a table!" he was saying as we crossed the courtyard, mimicking the motion with his hands. "At least a few centimeters off the ground, maybe more!"

The catacombs entrance looked like something right out of a fantasy book: an ancient stone arch with a thick wooden door and rusted bolts, sitting in the middle of the grass and unattached to any building. It was easy to imagine opening the door and stepping through into another world. Which was almost the case. Only it was more like the underworld.

The door revealed a steep staircase that led straight down into the earth. Torches hung on the wall, providing very dim light. At the bottom, a single tunnel led us in the opposite direction, directly under the church. It ended in a sort of cavern that wasn't very big, maybe twice the size of my bedroom back in Ohio, but with a high domed ceiling. And the whole thing was made out of bones.

They had been carefully organized: thick femurs forming the borders, pointed ribs protruding along the curve into the ceiling, and long, thin arm bones mixed with slender finger bones to create a macabre pattern. And *skulls*, skulls with hollow eyes and eerie grins, grouped into circles every few feet in a way that mirrored the stained glass windows up in the church.

"One day, when I have my own apartment," I murmured, "this is exactly how I'm going to decorate it."

Jamie laughed. "With real bones? Or, like, catacomb wallpaper?"

"Real bones, obviously," I said. "It's got to be authentic."

In the center of the cavern was a large, round table with about a dozen chairs around it. Professor Guzmán led everyone over and began taking a bunch of items out of his bag. Oscar and I hung back with Jamie and Hailey as the others took their seats, with the exception of Guzmán's student, who stood at his side, and Roland, who was walking around the room, peering closely at the bones like he was searching for something hidden between them.

Jamie nudged me. "You guys should be over there," he whispered. "You're part of the cast now."

"Not enough chairs," I said. "And we aren't filming, anyway." He shrugged and smiled. His arm kept grazing mine, and I couldn't help wondering if it was on purpose.

"Here it is," Professor Guzmán said grandly, waving a thick leather notebook in the air. "Brunilda Cano's journal.

Just one of the many treasures I found last year when cleaning out my grandmother's attic. All in Spanish, of course, but I translated an entry to give you an example." He handed Jess a printout. On either side of her, Lidia and Dad leaned closer. Sam just closed his eyes. I pulled out my Elapse, made sure the flash was off, and started taking pictures as Jess read out loud.

"*I fear not for my safety, but for the safety of those around me. The evil that has my soul in its claws will not loosen its grip; on the contrary, the exorcism seems only to have strengthened its resolve. Every day, I feel less myself. Every day, I see unspeakable things, things no one else can see, and I know they are the work of this demon.*" Jess set the paper on the table and turned to Lidia. "Voiceover narration?"

Lidia nodded. "That's what I was thinking."

"Professor Guzmán, is there any way we could make copies of all these entries?" Jess asked. "I'd like to go through them and record Lidia reading a few before Friday, if possible."

"Absolutely," Guzmán replied. "Inés, can you take care of that tomorrow morning?" His student nodded, making a note in her planner. I zoomed in on her, adjusting the focus. She looked vaguely familiar, although I was too distracted to wonder why. Brunilda's words were really creepy, but I loved stuff like this . . . so why did I suddenly feel so unsettled?

"This is fascinating," Dad said, flipping through a few

more of the translated pages. "A first-hand account of possession. Look here, this part about seeing messages written in blood on the walls of the sacristy?" He nudged Jess. "Let's make sure we get some footage in there. In fact . . ." Dad squinted down at the pages. "Looks like she saw lots of 'messages' no one else could see, both inside and outside of the church. We should write a list, make sure we cover all these places."

They continued talking, but blood was rushing in my ears. Dazed, I let my camera fall at my side. I kept picturing the cave behind the waterfall, *I WANT OUT* scratched all over in the photos.

Looks like she saw lots of messages no one else could see.

"Kat?" Jamie had called my name, and I realized he and Hailey were staring at me. The adults were all focused on the journal, but I saw Mi Jin watching us. My heart started pounding too loud and too fast, and I was seized with the sudden certainty that something terrible was about to happen.

I sucked in a sharp breath when Oscar grabbed my arm. "We're going outside for a few minutes, okay?" he said to the table in general. "It's kind of crowded in here."

"Don't go too far," I heard Lidia say. Oscar was already guiding me out of the catacombs, down the tunnel, and up the stairs. Jamie and Hailey were right on our heels.

"What's wrong?" Hailey asked. I couldn't respond. My lungs had forgotten how to take in air.

"Kat's sick," Oscar said, still gripping my elbow as he pushed on the door.

Thump. It had only opened a few inches before slamming into something on the other side. Or, judging by the resulting yelp, some*one.*

"Sorry!" Oscar exclaimed, carefully pushing the door open the rest of the way. I wrenched my arm from his grasp and stumbled a few steps away from the entrance before sitting on the grass. I took deep gulps of the fresh, warm air, willing my heart to slow down. Slowly, my panic began to fade. But what had caused it? I was still trembling with fear and nothing frightening had even happened.

It was a few seconds before I realized Jamie was kneeling next to me, his blue eyes filled with concern. Oscar and Hailey stood a few feet away, along with a familiar boy and girl—the teenagers who had been with the tour group in the church earlier. But the rest of their group was nowhere in sight.

"Do you need some water?" Hailey asked anxiously, hovering at my side. The girl smiled down at me sympathetically.

"Your first time in the catacombs?" she asked, her words carrying the tiniest trace of an accent. "Thiago's claustrophobic, he almost passed out the first time we went down there."

"*Claus*-what?" Her brother's accent was quite a bit thicker. "I did not pass out."

"I know, that's why I said 'almost.'"

As my anxiety faded, my face grew warm with embarrassment. "I'm fine," I mumbled. "I just got . . . hot."

Oscar eyed me in a way that made it clear he didn't believe me, but thankfully, he didn't push it. I started to stand, and the girl reached out a hand to help me up.

"Thanks."

"Of course. I'm Abril, this is Thiago," she added. "Our sister Inés is Guzmán's teaching assistant. We saw you in the church earlier," she added to Oscar. "Telling off that jerk for laughing at the tour guide."

"Aw, you told somebody off and we missed it?" Hailey made a face. "Dang."

"It was very good," Thiago said to Oscar, grinning. It brought out a little dimple on the left side of his mouth. "Very funny."

"Oh." Oscar blinked. "Um. Thank you."

I stared at him. Was he actually blushing? Like a modest human being might? That was new.

"You're with the TV show, right?" Abril asked. "*Passport to Paranormal*?"

"Yeah," I said, taken aback. "You've heard of it?"

"I studied abroad in California last year," Abril explained. "The family I lived with, they watched it sometimes. Professor Guzmán is very excited you're filming an episode about Brunilda."

Thiago's expression darkened when his sister mentioned

the professor's name. He started to say something, but Abril shot him a warning look.

Hailey must have noticed it, too. "What?" she asked eagerly. "You don't like Professor Guzmán?"

"No, it's . . . ," Abril said with a sigh. "He is . . . was . . . Inés's favorite professor. This Brunilda experiment, it was a risk for him. The university doesn't take it very seriously."

"But he's getting amazing results," Jamie pointed out. "He said that two weeks ago, Brunilda made the table *float*. They still aren't taking him seriously?"

Abril glanced back at the entrance. "No, they aren't. Inés thinks the university is going to stop funding all his projects, actually. They don't approve of what he's doing. That's why he's so happy your show is here. Good publicity for the school—he thinks it might save his job."

Oscar and I exchanged a glance. "I don't know about that," Oscar said slowly. "I mean, it's a ghost-hunting show. Half the fans don't even believe most of it."

"Some of them think we fake stuff," I added. Abril's eyes widened.

"Do you?"

"No," I said quickly. "The viewers are kind of on the lookout for it, you know? If they thought we were trying to trick them, I think a lot would just stop watching. The network's already warned us about it."

Abril's mouth was set in a thin line, but she said nothing. After a few seconds of fidgeting, Thiago turned to his sister.

"*¡Díles que Guzmán es mentiroso!*" he told her, his voice low and urgent. Grimacing, Abril started to respond, but Oscar beat her to it.

"Professor Guzmán's lying?" he said, looking back and forth between them. "About what?"

Thiago's eyes widened. "*¿Hablas español?*" He sounded delighted, but Oscar shook his head.

"Not really. I mean, I understand some. But I can't, um . . ."

"He speaks Portuguese," I told Thiago, because Oscar looked all flustered again. "What's Guzmán lying about?"

"The table . . ." Thiago lifted his hands like a puppeteer. "*Flotando.* Floating."

"And everything else that happens during the séances. But we can't prove it." Abril cast another nervous glance at the entrance. "We went into the catacombs with the tour group, then I stayed down there when they left. Thiago waited up here to tell me when you all were coming. I searched all over, looking for evidence that he's faking it, but . . . nothing."

"Why do you think he's faking?" Jamie asked.

"Inés thinks he is," Abril said. "She said it started out fine, but in the last month they've been reading the final entries in Brunilda's journal, the entries about her possession. That's when things got . . . violent." She waved her hands. "Not *violent*. But . . . objects flying, chairs and tables lifting, cold temperatures. That was also around the time the university told Professor Guzmán he had two months left before they stopped funding his research."

"But that doesn't mean he's faking it," Jamie said. "Maybe Inés doesn't believe in ghosts, but we've seen plenty of—"

"She *does*, though," Abril interrupted. "She believes in ghosts. But she says what's been happening during the séances . . ." She glanced at Thiago, who shrugged. "She says it's obviously fake. You'll see for yourself on Friday."

I let out a long, slow breath. "Yeah, when we film it. And show it on TV."

I could tell the others were thinking the same thing. The show's fans would always argue about whether little things, like our Ouija board experience, were real. But if we aired a whole episode about Guzmán's séance and the entire thing turned out to be fake, it would be disastrous for *Passport to Paranormal*.

To: acciopancakes@mymail.net
From: trishhhhbequiet@mymail.net
Subject: ARE YOU STILL ALIVE OR WHAT?!

um. hello?? haven't heard from you in like three days!!! D:

TELLING the rest of the cast the news about Guzmán didn't quite get the reactions Oscar and I were expecting.

"He's not faking anything," Lidia said immediately. "That's just what skeptics say when they face true paranormal activity."

Sam nodded in agreement. "There was a presence in the catacombs with us. I sensed her."

"Sorry, Sam, but *sensing a presence* won't mean squat to Thomas Cooper," Jess replied, massaging her temples with her fingers. Dad watched her, his brow furrowed.

"You think we should back out?" he asked.

"No." Jess hesitated. "In fact, if none of Guzmán's students have found any evidence, maybe we should just . . . ignore this."

Lidia's brows shot up. "What?"

"It's too late to find another place to investigate." Jess crossed her arms. "We can't back out. If he's faking it, he's clearly doing a great job, so . . ."

"So you think we should air it regardless." Lidia laughed dryly. "As long as it's entertaining, who cares if it's real, right?"

Oscar and I glanced nervously at one another. Jess believed in ghosts just as much as Lidia, but she'd always been more concerned with putting together a good show. Like the trick lightbulb in the pilot episode—I was willing to bet Jess and Roland had planned that without telling Lidia or Sam.

"I do care," Jess told Lidia. "I also care about getting canceled. Our ratings are getting better, but we're still on shaky ground with Fright TV. Look, you just said you believe Guzmán, so what's the problem? We're in agreement here."

"But for different reasons," Lidia muttered. An uncomfortable silence descended, broken by Dad.

"We do need to consider how we're going to handle it if it *does* turn out Guzmán is faking it," he pointed out. "I want to believe him, too, but just in case . . ."

Roland, who'd been silent since Oscar and I had finished telling everyone what we'd learned, finally spoke up.

"If it's real, great," he said flatly. "And if he's faking it, we just expose him during filming. Either way, it'll be one hell of an episode."

It was a fair point, I thought. Our more skeptical fans would probably love an episode where we exposed a fake haunting. So long as it didn't look like we were the ones faking it.

The meeting ended quickly after that. Even though everyone agreed with Roland, the atmosphere was still pretty tense. I holed myself up in Dad's and my room with his laptop and logged into my e-mail account.

To: trishhhhbequiet@mymail.net, timelord2002@mymail.net
From: acciopancakes@mymail.net
Subject: Re: ARE YOU STILL ALIVE OR WHAT?!

I'M SORRY I'M SORRY I'M SORRY! It's been a weird couple of days. How's winter break going? Trish, are you in Florida for the holidays? Mark, is your mom baking those peppermint brownies? And can you mail a hundred or so to Buenos Aires?

Lots to catch you guys up on. Long story, but I found out today that the professor we're featuring on the next episode—the one I mentioned in my blog post who says he's been contacting Brunilda Cano's ghost—might be faking it. One of his students thinks he is, anyway. And her brother and sister have been digging around for weeks trying to prove it but they can't. Soooo . . . this episode should be interesting.

The catacombs are awesome—I'll post some pictures tonight. We're making another video for that web series tomorrow (woo) (/sarcasm). We decided to try contacting Brunilda. In her journal, she mentions this big willow tree in the woods behind the church where she liked to sit and read, so we're going to take the Ouija board back there and give it a shot. Hopefully it'll turn out as good as the first video.

I drummed my fingers on the desk, thinking. Then, after glancing quickly around my empty hotel room, I started to type fast, without giving myself time to stop and think.

Speaking of, funny story: I think Ana Arias might be possessing me. Or at least haunting me. Ever since Oscar and I contacted her, I've been getting anxiety attacks. At first I thought it was stage fright because I hate being on camera with the fiery passion of a million suns. But it can't be just that, because it's happening when we're not even filming. And I've seen Ana a couple of times. I saw her at the waterfall and she looked right at me and waved. Then I saw her again—she's on a video I took of myself practicing so I wouldn't be so nervous on camera. She's in the mirror behind me, just for a second. Sam said she'd have to be really unsettled about something to leave her mother and follow me. But I can't figure out what she wants. Oscar and I found a bunch of articles about her and Flavia, but there's just not that much personal information about Ana. Her mom did a really good job protecting her from the media. Anyway, when we contacted Ana on the Ouija, she said, "I WANT OUT," right? Then I saw the same words all over the walls of the cave in my photos. But the words weren't actually there. And guess what a symptom of possession is? SEEING THINGS THAT AREN'T THERE. Brunilda saw "unspeakable things no one else can see." Lidia saw Red Leer's SHIP when he possessed her. Right now, the only thing keeping me from totally freaking out is that I only saw that message on my camera. Levi did some weird stuff to my camera back in Crimptown—maybe Ana altered my cave photos or something? Maybe she's not possessing me. But then again, Lidia was sick and acting all weird when she was possessed, and I keep getting these stupid panic attacks, and Oscar keeps saying I look sick. So maybe she IS possessing me?

Either way, Ana is definitely trying to tell me something, and I have no idea what.

I stopped, reading over my ramble. Then I started giggling.

I sounded *nuts*. Really, certifiably nuts. But the sad thing was, I meant every word.

Pulling the memory stick out of my pocket, I slid it into the laptop and opened the video of me talking into the camera. My finger hovered over the space bar, waiting, waiting . . . "*Just. Freaking. Relax.*" I tapped it quickly, and the video froze.

I leaned close to the screen, staring at the shape in the mirror. It was like a blurry shadow running between screen-me and the camera. Most of the pictures I'd seen of Ana showed her in a hospital gown, a scarf covering her bald head. But she'd had longer hair before the chemo treatments. If I squinted, this shadow kind of looked like she had a long ponytail.

I heard Dad's voice in the hall and quickly closed the video, stuffing the memory stick safely back in my pocket. I waved when he came in, and he put his hand over his cell phone. "Almost done?" he mouthed, pointing to the laptop.

"One minute," I promised, and he nodded before stepping back into the hall. Quickly, I deleted the bit with my ridiculous rant about being possessed and finished my e-mail.

> Glad you guys liked the waterfall episode! I kind of hate being on TV. Like a lot. But I guess I should just try to enjoy it. Oscar sure is. Did you read his *Rumorz* interview?
> Still haven't figured out a way to tell my mom I don't want to be a part of the Wedding from Hell. Maybe I'll try a compromise—tell her I'll be a bridesmaid, but only if she lets me

wear a dress made out of spiderwebs, like in *The Coven's Curse*. Grandma would be on board for sure. But Mom would never go for it, and then I'd be off the hook. Right? (No? Any other ideas would be appreciated.)

Miss you both,

Kat

I clicked *Send*, then flopped down on my bed. Dad came back in a few seconds later, still on the phone. I grabbed my headphones and iPod and scrolled through my movie selection until I found *The Coven's Curse*. An hour later I was sound asleep, dreaming of spider-silk bridesmaid dresses and a featureless girl with red-and-orange flames where her eyes should have been.

Inbox: (1 New!)
Subject: Monica tagged you in a photo album!

I **GLARED** at my phone, wiping the crusty sleep gunk from the corners of my eyes. No response from Trish and Mark yet. More wedding stuff from my mom. So far, this morning was not the best.

Despite my better judgment, I clicked on the link to Mom's album. This one was called *Fifteen weeks and counting!* To my relief, it was mostly pictures of things like flower arrangements and decorations. No photos of me in ill-fitting dresses. I imagined what kbold04 would say about those and suppressed a shudder.

"Wedding planning?"

I jumped about a foot at the sound of Dad's voice, then slammed the laptop shut. "No! It's . . . um . . ."

Dad laughed a little. "Honey, calm down. It's okay."

"She sent me a link," I explained, feeling dumb and guilty at the same time. "She keeps doing that, like I care what kind of cake she's getting or whatever."

"You know," Dad said slowly, sitting on the edge of the

bed. "It's okay if you *do* care. It's your mother's wedding."

I snorted. "I *don't* care. I don't even know why . . ." I stopped, staring down at my knees. I could feel Dad's eyes on me. "Wouldn't it bother you? Me being a bridesmaid for her? Because I won't do it if you don't want me to."

"Kat, look at me."

Grimacing, I forced myself to look up.

Dad took a deep breath. "I know you're still angry at her, and I know you've been trying to work on it. Whether or not you're in her wedding is entirely your decision—I'll support you either way. But I need you to know that you being a part of your mother's life isn't betraying me at *all*. Okay?"

"Okay," I mumbled. He got to his feet, kissed the top of my head, and said, "Breakfast?"

"Yeah."

"One minute, just gotta brush my teeth."

As soon as the bathroom door had closed behind Dad, I clicked over to my blog to check the comments on my post about the catacombs. "Seventy-three," I murmured. "Hooray." I scrolled quickly, not bothering to read the ones of my friends and the regular forum fans who commented. My stomach tightened as I got closer to the bottom. Sure enough, there he was.

kbold04: maybe ur the 1 whos possessed. or do u always look that disgusting

kbold04: can't beleive u r deleting all my comments like thats gonna stop me haha

kbold04: r u a zombie? a zombie wearing a zombie shirt? lol

He'd left thirty-one comments this time. They got progressively worse as they went along. I deleted them, but not after saving a screenshot of each one to add to my collection. I knew it was stupid to let one random person get to me this much. A stranger, someone whose opinion shouldn't even matter to me. And that's all it was— opinions, not threats. This wasn't like the letters Emily sent Sam, which (according to Roland) had gotten increasingly threatening. If this person was sending me stuff like that, I'd tell someone. But these comments . . . they were just words. Words I didn't want anyone else to see. I could handle it by myself.

Dad and I didn't talk much on the way downstairs. Trolls aside, I felt stupid for bringing the bridesmaid thing up with him. It's not like I ever thought for a second my dad would actually tell me he didn't want me in the wedding. I guess I just wanted someone else to make the decision for me, because I kept having the conversation with Mom in my head, and I got stuck in the same place every time.

Mom, I don't want to be in your wedding.

Why not?

Because you and Dad just got divorced, and it's weird. That wasn't entirely true. I mean, it *was* really fast. But they'd

128

been separated for half a year before the divorce. Mom's engagement had shocked me at first, but that wasn't what was really bothering me.

Because when you try to "girlify" me, it makes me feel like I'm not good enough. That *was* true. In fifth grade I'd been so excited about Halloween that I woke up Thursday, thought it was already Friday, and wore my zombie-clown costume to school. That whole day, I felt exactly like I did all the times Mom dressed me up: Everyone laughed when they saw me, but they also said lots of nice things about how great I looked, and then I spent the rest of the day feeling weird walking around dressed all funny when everybody else was just themselves. But that wasn't what was really bothering me, either. I could deal with dresses and makeup for a day, even if they made me feel awkward.

Because I don't see why I should be a part of your wedding when I'm not a part of your family. That was it. Mom used to have a husband and a daughter, but she kept leaving because she wasn't happy. Now she had a different soon-to-be husband and a different soon-to-be daughter, and she was the happiest I'd ever seen her. Why bother reinserting myself into the picture after she'd cut me out of it?

The problem was, every time I mentally said this to Mom, my eyes got all hot and watery. If I couldn't say it in my head without crying, no way could I get through it for real.

Maybe I could tell her in an e-mail via emojis.

"What's so funny?" Dad asked as we walked into the breakfast room.

"Nothing." I pressed my lips together.

After topping my stack of pancakes off with a waffle, I joined Oscar, Jamie, and Hailey at a table in the corner. We spent most of the next twenty minutes making plans for the video we were shooting this afternoon. Abril and Thiago were meeting us at the catacombs entrance, and then we were going to find the giant willow tree Brunilda mentioned in her journal. Lidia had loved the idea of featuring a few local kids in the web series, and she'd called their parents to get their permission and sent them a release waiver to sign.

At Jess's suggestion, I'd written a short outline like she did before shooting every episode. It described how to start and end the video and what "scenes" I envisioned. Once again, I found myself kind of enjoying the work Jess and Dad did to prepare for shows. I was hoping that sharing camera time with five other people instead of just one would make this a more fun experience.

I was so caught up in what we were doing that I didn't realize Mi Jin wasn't with the rest of the cast at the table next to us. Not until she appeared in the entrance, cleared her throat loudly, and said: *"Ta-da!"*

Glancing up, I choked on a mouthful of orange juice. Mi Jin stood there, arms outstretched, beaming. And she was *bald*.

Okay, not completely bald. More like a buzz cut, a soft fuzz of black still covering her head. She was wearing a little more eyeliner than usual, and her brow piercing really stood out now that she didn't have bangs. Her cheekbones looked sharper, too, somehow. Or maybe that was just because she was smiling so hard.

"Gorgeous!" Jess exclaimed, just as Roland whistled. Lidia, whose mouth was full, gave her two thumbs-up, and Dad applauded. Sam squinted at Mi Jin for a few seconds before his expression cleared.

"Ah," he said. "You shaved your head, right?"

Mi Jin snickered. "Keen observation as always, Sherlock." She walked over to our table and squatted between Jamie and me. "Looks like I've rendered Hailey speechless, but I'm not sure if that means she loves it or hates it."

I glanced at Hailey and giggled. Her eyes were bugged out and she was digging her fingers into her cheeks, her mouth open in a silent scream.

"That means she hates it," said Jamie immediately, which broke Hailey out of her trance.

"I do *not*," she hissed, punching her brother's arm. "It's just . . . I . . . why did you do that? Not that I don't like it!" she added hastily when the rest of us started laughing.

"I was telling Kat the other day that I shaved my head in high school," Mi Jin explained. "I realized I couldn't even remember why I ever let it grow back." She plucked a piece of bacon off Jamie's plate. "Plus it's super hot here, so."

"I think it looks great," said Oscar, and Jamie and I nodded in agreement.

131

Hailey tilted her head. "I *do* like it," she said at last, her tone decisive. "It looks really . . . soft. Can I feel it? Or is that weird?"

"Asking someone if you can rub their head?" Jamie asked. "No, that's not weird at all." Hailey stuck her tongue out at him, and Mi Jin grinned.

"Maybe later when you don't have sticky syrup hands."

She stood up and started to head over to the buffet. Hailey leaned closer, lowering her voice. "I can't believe she did that!" she whispered. "I wonder what all the fans will say when they see her in the next episode?"

Glancing over at Mi Jin, I smiled. "I'm pretty sure she doesn't care what they think," I told Hailey before digging back into my pancakes. Suddenly, this morning didn't seem so bad after all.

Hailey led the way into the woods behind the church, occasionally stopping to consult the pages in her hand. Inés had given us an extra copy of Brunilda's journal entries, all translated into English, and Hailey had immediately gone through and found all the ones with a description of Brunilda's favorite tree. She seemed to be taking charge of finding it, which was fine by me. Inés had also made a copy of Professor Guzmán's photo of the church's convent in 1891. He'd circled Brunilda's face: long and narrow like his, with a thin, pointed nose.

Jamie and I walked with Abril, who was filling us in on everything she knew about Professor Guzmán's experiment. "Inés has been his student for three years," Abril explained. "He's the only psychology professor at the university who is interested in telepathy, precognition, things like that. Last year when his grandmother died, he found this trunk in her attic with Brunilda Cano's belongings and personal records, and he learned she was a nun at this church."

"So Brunilda wasn't famous?" I asked.

"Famous?" Abril frowned. "No, she was just a nun."

"No, I mean her ghost."

"Most of the haunted places we visit are local legends," Jamie added. "All the locals know all about the ghosts and their stories."

Abril shook her head. "Everyone always said the catacombs were haunted, but no one had ever heard of Brunilda until Professor Guzmán started these séances."

Oscar and Thiago followed us, lagging behind a little bit. It sounded like Thiago was trying to teach Spanish to Oscar. Or maybe Oscar was trying to teach him Portuguese. I couldn't really tell.

"*As catacumbas são assombrados.*"

"*Assombrados?*"

"It means *haunted*. Haunted? *Com fantasmas?*"

"Ah . . . *embrujado.*"

Abril sighed loudly. "You should be working on your English, like I am!" she called over her shoulder. "He is very self-conscious about it," she added to Jamie and me. "But he'll study abroad the year after next like I did. He needs to *practice.*" She yelled the last part, and behind us, Thiago muttered something that sounded like "*mandona.*" Abril rolled her eyes as he and Oscar snickered.

"I don't care if you think I'm bossy," she said haughtily, shooting him a glare. "You know I'm right."

"All right, we'll practice English," Oscar said. I glanced back as he pointed at a spindly-looking tree. "Tree," he deadpanned, and Thiago started laughing again.

"I see it!" Up ahead, Hailey broke into a run. Our narrow path opened into a small clearing, and a massive willow tree stood in the center, leaves swaying gently in the breeze. I stopped, setting my Elapse to video mode and holding it a few inches from my face. On the display screen, Hailey sprinted toward the tree, ponytail flying. Jamie leaned closer to watch. Maybe a little closer than necessary. Not that I was complaining about that.

"That'll be a nice opening shot," he said, his breath tickling my cheek. I nodded, pretty sure that if I tried to respond, it would come out as a squeak.

Jamie stuck by my side as I filmed the others setting up the Ouija board. His arm kept accidentally brushing against mine, and once when I tripped over a root, he grabbed my wrist and held onto it several seconds after I'd regained my balance. The resulting swooping sensation in my stomach, combined with my now-typical anxiety that came with filming, made me feel like I was on a roller coaster that was sort of fun but also sort of terrifying. By the time Oscar was ready for the introduction, my hands were sweating and a soundtrack of *thump-thump, thump-thump* was playing loudly in my ears.

I tried to hold the camera steady as he talked about Brunilda, but something was wrong. A buzzing noise filled my ears, drowning out Oscar's words, and neon spots started flickering in front of my eyes. For a second, I swore I saw a shape through the viewfinder. One that looked a whole lot like the shape I'd seen in the mirror.

"Kat?" Someone gently took the camera from my hands. I took a deep, shaky breath, blinking rapidly.

"What are you doing?"

Jamie frowned slightly. "I was talking to you. Didn't you hear me?"

"Oh sorry." I shook my head, trying to get rid of the buzzing noise. "I'm just, um, distracted."

"Do you mind if I film this part?" Jamie held up the Elapse.

"No, but why?"

"Just want to try it." Pretending to inspect the back of the camera, Jamie lowered his voice. "And because you look like you did in the catacombs yesterday, like you're going to faint. If you don't want to talk about whatever's going on, that's fine, but I thought you might want to get some water and sit down for a minute."

I swallowed. "Okay. Thanks."

"No problem." He glanced up at me, a smile crinkling the corners of his eyes. "Although, you know, if you ever *do* want to talk about it . . ."

I couldn't help smiling back. "Yeah, maybe later."

Trying to look nonchalant, I headed over to my backpack and sat cross-legged on the grass. Rocks littered the area around the tree, dark gray and shiny. I picked one up and examined the marbled pattern, half listening as Oscar interviewed Abril. Should I tell Jamie about the whole Ana Arias thing? I knew it would hurt Oscar's feelings if I confided in Jamie but not him. But if Oscar knew I suspected Ana was following us—if he knew she might even be possessing me—he'd find a way to get the whole story on the show, even if I resisted. Just like with the web series.

When Oscar and Abril finished, Jamie filmed Hailey reading an entry from Brunilda's journal. I sat with my eyes closed, turning the rock over and over in my hand as I listened.

"The willow tree behind the church has long been a favorite spot of mine to read and be alone with my thoughts. But even this place, it seems, is no longer safe. I see the shadow in the church nearly every day now, dancing and writhing in the corner of my eye, always vanishing when I turn to get a better look. Only in the church, though . . . until this morning, when I visited my willow tree."

I rubbed my arms, my skin prickling with goose bumps

despite the heat. When Hailey finished reading, everyone moved to sit around the Ouija board. Reluctantly, I pulled the tripod from my backpack and set it up before taking the Elapse from Jamie. (I'd tried "forgetting" the tripod back at the hotel so that I'd have to film the séance rather than be on camera, but Oscar had helpfully reminded me.)

After turning the camera on, I adjusted the angle, trying to get everyone in the shot. I kept thinking of the shadow I'd seen in the viewfinder a few minutes ago and wondering if I'd imagined it. Imagined *her*. "Ana Arias," I murmured to myself as I tightened the base of the tripod. "Why are you following me?"

I squeezed between Jamie and Hailey and placed my fingers on the planchette. As usual, Jamie took charge of the séance. Closing my eyes, I tried to focus on his voice and not on the quiet *whir* coming from the camera.

"Brunilda Cano used to sit under this willow tree and write in her journal," he began. "Hailey's going to read the rest of that entry, and I want everyone to imagine Brunilda right here with us. Concentrate on her words, her thoughts, her emotions."

There was a long silence, and I peeked through my eyelashes. Hailey sat solemnly, staring at the journal in her lap. When she spoke, her voice was much softer than usual.

"The monster followed me here, lurking just out of sight, revealing itself only when I sat beneath the willow.

I looked up and saw it hanging there in the branches,
hollow-eyed and smiling."

A chill raced up my spine. I had to resist the urge to tilt
my head back and stare up into the branches. But I could
imagine it there, some shadowy thing lurking behind the
leaves, watching us. Watching me.

"I realized this monster is always with me, and always
has been. It's not trying to hurt me; it's protecting me. It's
not trying to steal my soul; it's trying to save it."

Terror seized me. My heart was hammering so loudly, I
could barely hear Hailey. I sat frozen, suddenly positive that
if I opened my eyes, I would see . . . something. Brunilda's
empty-eyed monster grinning down at us. Or maybe Ana
Arias, covered in dirt from her grave. Dozens of horrifying
images flickered through my mind but I knew, I just *knew*,
that whatever was with us right now was worse.

Hailey continued reading, her voice trembling a little.
Dimly, I wondered if she'd realized a monster had joined
our group right there in broad daylight.

"The clergy wants to perform an exorcism. I think I
mustn't let them. I think perhaps it would be best if this
beast stayed with me."

The planchette began to crawl slowly, slowly across the board.

Hailey fell silent. I forced myself to open my eyes, but my vision was blurry. The buzzing noise was back, too. I sensed it, whatever it was we'd conjured, hovering between the camera and me. But I was too petrified to look at it. All I could do was stare at my fingers, which felt magnetically attached to the planchette.

"I . . . ," Jamie said as our hands stopped over the letter briefly, then moved on to the next. "W . . . A . . . N . . ."

Stop, I wanted to scream.

"T . . ."

Oscar said something I couldn't make out through the deafening rush of blood in my ears. But I knew what he was saying, because I was thinking it, too. We both knew what the final three letters would be.

Without thinking, I yanked my hands away from the planchette and crawled backward away from the board in a panic. There was a shout and a cry, and then I bumped into something. I looked up, and for a single, heart-stopping second, I expected to be staring right into the face of some sort of demon.

But it was just my camera.

It fell off the tripod and landed in my lap, the lens retracting as it shut off. I could see my reflection in the black viewfinder: disheveled, sweaty, panicked.

What was *wrong* with me?

Suddenly, I felt ridiculous. The last few minutes replayed in my mind, and I couldn't understand why I'd been so scared. No, more than scared—*petrified*. I'd seen ghosts before. I saw Sonja Hillebrandt and the prisoners at Daems. I saw Lidia possessed by Red Leer. Emily Rosinski held a knife to my throat, for crying out loud, and that had been scarier than any paranormal activity I'd ever experienced. So why had I been so terrified sitting under a tree in the middle of the afternoon with my friends? It wasn't like me.

Maybe it *wasn't* me.

I finally looked up at the others, expecting to find them staring at me like I belonged in a straitjacket. But only Oscar and Jamie were watching me. Hailey was hugging her knees and gazing at the planchette, her expression troubled. At some point, Thiago must have gotten frightened, because he now stood several feet away from the board, arms crossed. Abril got to her feet and went over to talk to him, and he started shaking his head.

"Sorry," I finally managed to say, scooting back toward Jamie. "I don't know why I freaked out like that."

He shook his head. "I know. I've never had that happen during Ouija before."

For a second, I thought he meant my panic attack, and I wanted to sink into the ground in humiliation. Then I realized Jamie looked shaken, too. In fact, everyone did.

"I actually got *cold*," Hailey said, brow furrowed. "I was so scared, and now I don't know why. I felt . . . *lost*."

Jamie nodded in agreement, and a wave of relief washed over me. They'd felt it, too. Maybe I wasn't losing my mind after all.

"Kat," Oscar said quietly, and I looked up at him. "It spelled *I want.*"

The relief vanished as quickly as it had come, and my stomach sank. "Yeah . . ."

"That message we got from Ana . . ."

"Yeah."

He pushed the bangs out of his eyes, frowning. "Why, though? Why would Brunilda say the same thing?"

I didn't respond. I was afraid that if I started talking about it, the whole story would spill out: seeing Ana at the waterfall, seeing the message in the cave. But how much longer could I keep this to myself?

"Well," said Jamie at last. "I'm sure when you post this video, the fans will come up with tons of theories."

"They're going to think it's just a stunt," Oscar said immediately. "Getting the same message twice like that."

"We don't know for sure this message would have been the same." I shoved the Elapse in my pocket. "She didn't get to finish it this time. Anyway, I'm getting pretty tired of worrying about what people think. Let's post it."

After dinner, Jess offered to help Oscar and me edit our video. I promised to meet them, along with Jamie and

Hailey, in fifteen minutes. Then I returned to my room and sprawled out on my bed.

Exhaustion weighted my bones in a way that made me wonder, vaguely, if I was coming down with something. My last thought before I drifted off was that Lidia took a lot of naps when she was possessed. But I was currently too tired to feel frightened.

When I opened my eyes again, my room was pitch black. Stifling a groan, I rolled over and squinted at the alarm clock: *3:36 a.m.* I could barely make out the lump that was Dad in the other bed, snoring deeply.

My limbs felt stiff and sore as I pushed the blankets off. I was still wearing my shorts and *Gremlins* shirt; Dad must have found me napping and tucked me in. So I'd gone to bed at 8:30 p.m. That was kind of embarrassing. But my throat was dry and aching. Maybe I really was getting sick.

I shuffled to the bathroom and groped around the counter until I found a glass. I filled it with water from the sink, blinking and gazing at the faucet. It was hard to tell in the dark, but it looked like the silver was scratched. So was the mirror, actually.

Suddenly, I was wide-awake. Clutching my glass in one hand, I fumbled for the light switch. The fluorescent glare momentarily blinded me. When my eyes started to adjust, I wished I'd left the lights off.

The faucet, the marble counter, the mirror, the tile floor, and walls . . . everything was covered in scratches, deep gouges like from the claws of a wild animal. But no animal could have done this. Because the scratches spelled three words, over and over again.

I

WANT

OUT

CHAPTER ELEVEN
EXORCISE YOUR WAY TO BETTER HEALTH

P2P WIKI
Entry: "Exorcism"
[Last edited by AntiSimon]

The process of driving out a spirit, ghost, demon, or other being possessing a person, place, or thing. Though typically a religious ritual, exorcisms are occasionally secular. The ritual is conducted by an exorcist, who may use a variety of methods and objects to banish the spirit, most of which involve calling on some higher power. To date, *Passport to Paranormal* has never filmed an exorcism.

UPDATE: Many fans believe P2P participated in its first exorcism during the Daems Penitentiary episode (EP #30). Although not captured on camera, one popular theory states that Kat Sinclair played the role of the exorcist by using her camera to drive Red Leer's ghost from Lidia's body.

THE GLASS slipped from my hand, shattering on the floor. Someone screamed. No, not someone. *Me.*

Shards of glass crunched beneath my feet as I fled the bathroom. A pair of strong hands gripped my shoulders, and I sucked in a breath, ready to scream again.

"Kat!"

Dad's bloodshot eyes were wide with panic. I collapsed

x

against him, squeezing mine shut.

"What happened?" he asked, his voice unusually high. I'd never heard him sound this frightened before. Still holding me tightly, he leaned into the bathroom.

"I didn't do it." My words came out muffled against his chest.

"Honey, it's okay. It's just a broken glass, no big deal."

"What?"

Slowly, I pulled away from him and turned around. No words. No scratches. The mirror, the walls—everything was back to normal, except for the broken glass scattered on the tile floor.

I swallowed the lump in my throat and took a tentative step forward. "Ow!"

"Stop." Before I had time to respond, Dad swept me up and carried me over to the chair. He knelt in front of me, carefully inspecting the bottoms of my feet. "Don't move," he ordered. I sat with my legs hovering a few feet off the floor while he grabbed the first-aid kit he had stashed in the closet and turned on the lights.

"I don't feel anything" I said as he began picking tiny shards from my left foot. "Am I bleeding?"

"I don't think so," Dad replied, squinting. "Looks like there are a few tiny cuts, but it could've been worse." He glanced at me. "So . . . wanna tell me what happened?"

I squirmed when he started to apply ointment to one of the cuts. "I saw . . . I thought I saw something in the bathroom," I said at last. "Scratches."

Dad's brow furrowed. "Scratches?"

"On the walls and mirror. It . . ." *It spelled I WANT OUT.* I exhaled slowly. "It scared me and I dropped the glass."

He closed the first-aid kit and studied me. "It's not like you to see things."

"Yeah." *Because it's not me.*

"I can't remember the last time you had a nightmare," he said. "Especially one that made you scream like that. Scared the hell out of me."

"Sorry," I whispered. Then I realized what he'd said. "Nightmare? I wasn't asleep!"

"Well, there aren't any scratches in the bathroom, right?" Dad smiled a little. "You conked out really early, and *hard.* I knocked over my suitcase when I came in and you didn't even budge. Sounds to me like you were sleepwalking."

I started to shake my head, then stopped. What was the point of arguing? *Sure, maybe I was sleepwalking. Or maybe the ghost of a dead Brazilian singer's daughter, who might be possessing me, is making me see things. That's also a perfectly reasonable explanation, right?*

After we cleaned up the rest of the glass, Dad turned on the TV and found a sitcom. He claimed he was too awake and felt like watching something, but I knew he was doing it because he thought I was scared. Two minutes into the show and he was snoring as loud as ever. I lay awake, listening to the laugh track and counting the bumps on the ceiling.

In all honesty, I *was* scared. But not of the dark or of nightmares.

I was afraid of myself.

By the time I dragged myself out of bed, Dad was gone. I skipped showering—the memory of the scratches all over the tile was a little too fresh—and brushed my teeth and hair without looking in the mirror. When I got down to the lobby, Jamie was sitting on the sofa looking through a bunch of papers. He beamed when he saw me.

"Hey!"

"Hi!" I sat down, suddenly wishing I'd at least glanced at my reflection. "Where is everybody?"

"The church." Jamie held out a napkin-wrapped muffin. "Breakfast room closed a few minutes ago, so I grabbed this for you."

"Thanks." I took the muffin gratefully. "Sorry I didn't help edit last night."

"It's okay! Your dad said you crashed pretty early."

I picked off a piece of muffin but didn't eat it. "Yeah. I wasn't feeling good."

Jamie was silent for a moment. I waited, wondering if he was going to ask what was wrong, or why I was acting so weird lately. I still wasn't sure how much I wanted to share. Especially after last night.

"Oscar and I have a theory," he suddenly announced,

and my stomach turned over.

"About what?"

"You."

"Um. Okay?"

"So yesterday during Ouija, the message started out *I want*," Jamie began. I nodded, trying not to shiver at the words. "Which could have been the same message you got from Ana back in Salvador, *I want out*. We were thinking it's possible Ana came with you."

My face grew warm. "I've sort of wondered about that, too. Actually, I—I asked Sam and Roland about it because I kind of saw her at the waterfall."

Jamie's eyes widened. "You did? Oscar didn't mention that."

"I never told him," I admitted. "Anyway, Sam said she'd have to have a pretty big reason to leave her mother's grave and follow us, and I . . . I just have no idea why she'd do that."

"I do." Jamie leaned forward. "This is going to seem kind of out there, though."

"Probably no weirder than what I've been thinking." I tried to sound casual, but my stomach was knotting up tighter and tighter. Oscar and Jamie didn't even know about the message on the cave walls or in the bathroom. If they thought I was possessed, too . . .

"Okay." Jamie took a deep breath. "We think you might be an exorcist."

I gaped at him. "A . . . *what*?"

"You know, a person who performs exorcisms," he

explained eagerly. "After the Daems episode, everyone was freaking out about Emily. But some of the fans in the forums were more interested in what happened to Lidia. Especially after you blogged about Red Leer, how he'd been possessing her for, like, a week, how you'd gotten rid of him by using the flash on your camera. One person posted this theory: He thinks you basically performed an exorcism. Which is true, if you think about it," Jamie added. "An exorcism is forcing a spirit out of another person's body, right?"

I blinked a few times. Bizarre as the idea was, it *did* make sense.

"So last night, Oscar and I stayed up researching exorcisms," Jamie went on, speaking faster now. "Exorcists can get rid of spirits possessing people—*and* animals *and* objects. Theoretically, they can even sometimes send the spirit from one thing into another, like, to trap it. So we think maybe when you guys contacted Ana, you somehow used your camera to exorcise her, just like you did with Red Leer."

"From who?" I interrupted. "She wasn't possessing anyone!"

"Right," Jamie said. "But spirits can possess objects, too, remember? If her spirit was there—in her grave, her tombstone, or even her mother's tombstone—you might have, like, pried her loose or something." He paused, wrinkling his nose. "Okay, we don't totally have that part of the theory worked out yet. But the rest makes sense."

149

I smiled despite myself. "Sure it does."

Jamie grinned. "Just hear me out. Let's say somehow you conjured Ana's ghost out of her grave and transferred it to another object. Then you took that object along and carried it with you everywhere. A possessed object like that, with all that spirit's emotions, would make you feel weird, right? Anxious. Maybe even paranoid. And every time you used that object, the spirit would tell you what she wants: to *get out.*"

I sat up straight, the forgotten muffin rolling off my lap and onto the sofa. "Oh my God. You think Ana is in my *camera*?"

"Pretty much," Jamie said. "It would explain why you've been feeling sick; you're picking up on Ana's emotions. We all felt it yesterday when the camera was filming us. And it would explain why you've hated being around cameras in general."

That took a second to process. "How did you know about that?" I asked. It came out maybe a little more defensive than I intended.

"Oscar told me." Jamie looked a bit nervous. "I hope you don't mind—I asked him if he knew why you've been acting so weird. He said you thought you were camera shy or something, and you don't like being on TV. We just wanted to figure out what was going on so we could help."

"I don't mind," I said slowly. "I thought I had stage fright. But that kind of thing doesn't usually make me nervous."

"Exactly—because it was Ana, not you!" Jamie exclaimed.

Then his face fell. "Wait, but you saw Ana at the waterfall? That doesn't make sense if she's in your camera."

"Yes, it does." I closed my eyes, remembering the scene. "I saw her through the viewfinder. When I lowered the camera, she was gone." *And the cave! I only saw the message in the pictures, not on the actual cave walls.*

"Then we're right!" Jamie said excitedly. For a half second, my spirits lifted. Then I remembered the bathroom last night.

No camera.

Jamie was still watching me, so I did my best to look enthusiastic. "I think so, yeah! It makes a lot of sense." *Except at some point, Ana might have moved from the camera to me.* "So . . . so what should we do? How do we get her out of . . . um, my camera?"

"There's a library a few blocks from here," Jamie replied immediately. "Abril showed me. We can use their computers, since everyone took their laptops to the church; they're setting up all the equipment to film tonight. Oscar asked us to look up some stuff about Brunilda and the catacombs, too."

"Okay." As we headed across the lobby, I realized something. "Hey, where *is* my camera? I left it with you guys last night when you were uploading the video."

"Oscar has it," Jamie told me, holding the door open. "He and Hailey are going to go through Guzmán's stuff and see if they find any evidence that he's planning any tricks during the séance. But Oscar thought he'd try using your camera and seeing if he got any more messages or weird vibes, like yesterday."

"Ah." I wondered how I'd explain it when Oscar didn't see or feel anything unusual. *Funny thing, I don't think Ana's in there anymore . . .*

"Where *is* Oscar?" I asked suddenly. "He didn't want to come?"

Jamie gave me a sidelong glance as we crossed the street. "He did, but Hailey talked him into going with her and the cast so this would just be you and me."

"Why?"

"Well . . ." He looked down at his shoes, face slightly red. "For some reason, a few months ago Hailey decided she was really good at matchmaking. She spent all semester trying to fix up her friends at school and some of mine, too. Most of them did *not* appreciate it."

We turned the corner, walking past the east side of the church and the wrought-iron gates to a small cemetery. I could see the library a few blocks down, a small but stately gray building that looked more like a mansion.

"Anyway," Jamie continued, "the week before school let out, she kept leaving fake love notes from this girl, Tamara, in my friend Roger's locker, and fake notes from Roger in Tamara's locker, because she was convinced they liked each other." His mouth quirked up. "They did not. It was awkward."

I stifled a giggle. "That's kind of hilarious." Then I realized what he was implying, and a blush crept up my neck. "Wait, so . . . are you saying she's trying to set *us* up?"

"Yeah. I told her to knock it off," Jamie said quickly. "And that Oscar could come with us. But he said he didn't mind. Although he also said going to the library maybe wasn't the best place for a first date. Not that this is a date!" he added. "Unless, I mean . . . do you want it to be one?"

My skin started to tingle and my heart sped up, kind of like a sugar rush.

"Well," I said, trying to sound casual. "Figuring out how to perform an exorcism actually sounds like a pretty ideal first date to me."

I sneaked a glance at him. His cheeks were still pink, but he was smiling. "Works for me, too."

Nerves twisted my stomach, but mostly in a nice way. And besides, I was tired of being frightened: of cameras, of trolls, of ghosts. Of all the things that could scare me, I wasn't about to let *boys* be one of them.

So after only a second's hesitation, I reached out and took his hand, and neither of us let go.

All right, Ana, I thought to the dead girl who was maybe-probably possessing me. *No creepy messages for a few hours, okay? Be cool.*

The library wasn't all that big, but there was a whole room dedicated to local history and genealogy. The librarian helped me and Jamie log in to one of the computers, and we started looking up everything we could find about exorcisms, using an online language translator when necessary. We found a lot of weird stuff, including a hilarious interview Grandma had done for *Return to the Asylum* that even I'd never read before. After an hour, we hadn't found anything useful, but we were having too much fun to care.

While I didn't have the heart to tell Jamie, the more I thought about his theory, the more holes I found. How had I "exorcised" Ana in the first place? With Lidia, the camera flash caused her to have a seizure, which got rid of Red Leer. But nothing like that had happened at the graveyard. I'd been so nervous, not to mention mortified about the whole *I wonder what it would be like to have a mom who cared about me* thing I'd blurted out. I remembered sitting by Ana's tombstone and seething; thinking Oscar was trying to move the planchette, thinking about my mom and her wedding, thinking about how much I hated being on camera . . . Jamie always said you had to really focus on a spirit during Ouija, and I hadn't really been thinking about Ana at all.

Then there were my panic attacks. I desperately wanted to believe that I could blame all that anxiety on my camera, but I couldn't. The truth was, I'd been freaked out about being on TV since the moment Dad mentioned it on the plane. That was *my* anxiety, not Ana's.

What was it Roland had said? *Your brain is occupied with your own situation, and it projected your issues onto the idea of her.* But even that idea didn't quite work anymore. Jamie, Oscar, and all the others had felt it at the park yesterday: the presence of something. They'd all been anxious, too. Whatever was happening, it wasn't *entirely* inside my head.

"Wait, scroll back up," Jamie said, breaking me out of my thoughts. I scrolled up until he pointed. "That one. *The Four Basic Stages of an Exorcism.*"

I clicked the link, and we read silently for a minute.

The process of exorcizing a spirit can be broken down into four basic stages, as follows:
1. Concealment. The spirit keeps its identity and presence a secret.
2. Exposure. The spirit reveals its identity, either willingly or through force by the exorcist.
3. Confrontation. The exorcist confronts the spirit and attempts to force it out of the victim.
4. Banishment (or Reclamation). Either the exorcist is victorious, or the spirit reclaims the victim.

"That's how it was with Lidia," I said slowly. "She started acting strange, but we didn't know why. Next Red Leer 'revealed his identity' at Daems, when he made Lidia release the prisoners. Then I confronted him and banished him with the camera. All four stages."

"Right now, we're stuck at stage two," Jamie replied. "I mean, we *know* the spirit is Ana, but we haven't exposed her yet. I guess we've got to do that somehow before we can confront her."

"Yeah." I glanced at the clock in the corner of the screen. "We should probably start looking up Brunilda if we're supposed to meet with Oscar and Hailey at one." Opening the library catalog, I typed in *Brunilda Cano* and hit the search button.

No results found.

"Nothing?" I said, surprised. "The church did an exorcism on a nun and there's no record, no newspaper article?"

Jamie wrinkled his nose. "Huh. Maybe try the name of the church? The exorcism was in 1891, try that, too."

Nodding, I typed *Catedral de Nuestra Señora de la Encarnación, convento, 1891*. A few results popped up, including a link to a digitized microfilm photo, which I clicked immediately.

"Well, there's the photo," Jamie said, leaning closer to the screen. "That's her, right?"

He pointed to the sharp-faced nun in the first row, and I squinted. "Yeah, she's the one Guzmán circled. And there's . . . wait, hang on." I tapped the grainy, scanned caption clip next to the photo, where the nuns were listed in order from left to right. "Her name's not on here."

Jamie's brow furrowed. "Second from the left, first row . . . María Carmen Romero. Did they skip Brunilda?"

"Nope." I touched each face with my finger. "Seven nuns, seven names." I sat back, frowning. "Why does Guzmán think that's her?"

Neither of us spoke for a few seconds. Then Jamie

jumped up and grabbed my hand, pulling me out of my chair. "I have an idea."

We hurried out of the library and back up the street toward the church. But Jamie veered off into the cemetery, leading me to the first row of headstones behind the church.

"Is there a reason we're here?" I asked. "Not that cemeteries aren't excellent first-date venues, too . . ."

He laughed. "I'm looking for Brunilda's grave. She was a nun at this church, so she'd be buried here, right?"

"I guess, yeah." We wandered up and down the rows, still holding hands. The tombstones were old and weather-beaten, but the names and dates were still pretty legible. "Look, Sor María Carmen Romero . . . died November 28, 1891. The same day Brunilda Cano died, according to Guzmán."

Jamie gazed at the tombstone thoughtfully. "Did she change her name or something? Don't nuns sometimes do that?"

"Maybe," I said. "But if she was born Brunilda Cano, her name would've come up when we searched the library catalog. It would've been somewhere in the genealogy section."

"Good point."

We continued down the row, checking each grave. After a few minutes, Jamie pulled out his phone and checked the time. "Twenty to one," he said, making a face. "If we're going to check every tombstone, we should probably split up."

"I'll do the last two rows," I replied. "Meet you at the gate?"

"Okay."

I hurried down the path to the graves farthest from the church. As I slowed my pace to check each tombstone, I thought about that last exorcism article we'd found. I still had no idea how to actually conduct an exorcism. Half the stuff we found online was either obviously fake or obviously joking, and the rest suggested stuff like holy water and prayers, depending on the religion. The only thing they really had in common was the idea that the exorcist basically *convinced* the spirit to leave. Sometimes the fight turned physical, but usually words were enough.

But what was I supposed to say? And was it even possible for me to exorcise *myself*?

Five minutes later, I headed back to the cemetery entrance. Jamie stood waiting at the gate, hands behind his back. "Any luck?" he asked.

"Nope. You didn't find her, either?" When he shook his head, I frowned. "So the only records of Brunilda Cano even existing are just the stuff Guzmán found in his grandmother's attic? And in his photo, that's not even Brunilda . . . This is getting weird."

"Yeah, very." Jamie cleared his throat and held out a long brown stem. Several dried-up petals drooped from the end, yellowing and crinkly, like skinny, shriveled fingers. "For you."

"A dead flower?" I asked, confused. "Did you take that from someone's grave?"

His eyes widened. "No! I found it on the path—it must've fallen out of a bouquet or something. I thought, you know . . . first date. Flowers."

"Oh!" I exclaimed, flustered. "Thanks." I took the flower, trying not to smile too hard and failing pretty miserably. "Ooh, I think it's got a few strands of cobweb on it. How romantic."

"Gah, really?" Jamie wiped his hands on his shirt frantically, and I snickered. "Hey, I draw the line at spiders."

I inspected the lily, then held it out. "Spider-free, see?"

He leaned away, shaking his head. "I'll take your word for it."

We left the cemetery and headed inside the church, joking about spiders and other phobias. By the time we entered the courtyard, Jamie was telling me about how Hailey was deathly afraid of squirrels.

"Squirrels?" I repeated in disbelief. "I thought she wasn't afraid of anything!"

"That's what she wants everyone to think," Jamie said. "But yeah. She used to act kind of weird when we'd go to Central Park, but she wouldn't say why. Then this one time a squirrel ran across our picnic blanket, and Hailey actually tried to *kick* it. She missed, and the squirrel took off in one direction and Hailey ran the other way, screaming her head off." He paused, smiling sort of guiltily. "I got her a stuffed squirrel for Christmas last year."

I grinned. "Mean."

"Yeah. Especially considering I hid it at the bottom of her stocking so it was the last thing she pulled out."

"*Meaner,*" I said, laughing. Up ahead, the door to the catacombs stood slightly ajar. Oscar and Thiago were sitting shoulder to shoulder on the grass along the side, leaning against the crumbling stone. Thiago was talking animatedly, waving his hands in the air. As we got closer, I realized he was speaking English—and pretty well, too. Maybe he was more comfortable talking when his sister wasn't around. Oscar was listening intently, and both were totally oblivious to our presence.

"Hi," I said. They looked up, clearly startled. "Where's Hailey?"

"She asked Abril to take her to some market," Oscar replied.

Jamie frowned. "Why?"

"She didn't say. We were down there taking pictures of the catacombs and talking to Guzmán, and as soon as we got up here she said she had to go to . . . ah . . ." He looked at Thiago. "What's it called?"

"Plaza Dorrego."

"Oh right—I think that's where Mi Jin took her yesterday to get souvenirs," Jamie said. "Is it close?"

"Um . . ." Thiago gestured over his shoulder. "San Telmo is the neighborhood. Not very far. A few bus stops." His voice was much softer than it had been a minute ago, and he smiled shyly at us.

"She took the bus?" Jamie sounded rather alarmed.

"I'm gonna call her. She's not supposed to go off anywhere without telling me since Dad's in meetings all day." He walked a few steps away, pulling out his phone. I settled on the grass on Oscar's other side. He eyed the crusty dead flower as I laid it in my lap, mouth twitching like he wanted to laugh.

"How was your date?" He said it very, very quietly.

"Good." I said it very, very quietly, too. "How was yours?"

Oscar's eyes narrowed slightly, although not exactly in an angry way. More like in a *very-funny-but-seriously-shut-up-now* kind of way. So I did, arranging my face into an innocent expression as Jamie sat down with us.

"They just got off the bus," he said. "Should be here any minute. She wouldn't tell me what they were doing, though. What happened with Guzmán?"

"Nothing interesting, really," Oscar said. "He brought everything else of Brunilda's that he found in the trunk: a rosary, shoes, some old books, stuff like that. Here, I took pictures of it all." He pulled my Elapse out of his pocket and handed it to me. "I couldn't use it for very long though," he added. "I started feeling sick after a few minutes, just like at the park yesterday. I think everyone did. Guzmán didn't say anything, but even he looked kind of pale."

I gaped at him. "Are you serious?"

"Yeah . . ." Oscar's brow creased. "Why are you so surprised? You told her our Ana theory, right?" he added to Jamie, who nodded.

"I know, it's just . . ." I trailed off, gazing at the Elapse. Nothing made sense anymore. If my camera actually did have an effect on everyone's anxiety levels, maybe Ana really *was* possessing it. But then what about the scratches in the bathroom? What about all the panic attacks I had when my camera wasn't even on?

"You guys, you guys, you guys!" Hailey came sprinting toward the church, cheeks red with exertion. Abril followed a few seconds later, at a less frantic pace. Jamie opened his mouth when Hailey plopped down next to him, but she waved at him to be quiet before he could say a word.

"Yeah, I know, I was supposed to call you, but whatever, Jamie, I was with Abril and she knows where she's going and it's not like Dad's even gonna care. *Anyway.*" Hailey took a deep, shaky breath. "Oscar, you took a picture of Brunilda's journal, right?"

"Yup. Several."

Hailey grabbed the Elapse out of my lap and flipped it on. She scrolled through a few photos, then turned the viewfinder so we could see. "Okay, look at it really closely," she said, flipping to the next picture, and then the next. "Leather cover. Look at the stitching, the red-and-yellow pattern. And then here, the initials *BC* engraved in a bronze plate in the corner. Look at the shape of the plate—like a sand dollar, right?"

I leaned closer. "Right . . ."

Turning the camera off, Hailey stuck her hand in the

little purse slung across her shoulders. "In other words, it looks exactly like . . . *this*."

She pulled a leather journal out with a flourish, beaming proudly. For a moment, we all stared at it: the red-and-yellow stitching, the bronze sand-dollar plate with the initials *BC*. Jamie made a move to grab it, but Hailey held it out of his reach.

"Did you take that from Guzmán?" he exclaimed, and she shook her head and smiled.

"Nope. Check it out." Hailey opened the journal and held it so we could watch as she flipped through the pages. "Blank. It's brand new."

"There's a small shop that sells handmade leather journals, bags, things like that," Abril explained. She looked almost as excited as Hailey. "El Dólar de Arena. The Sand Dollar."

"I saw it when I was with Mi Jin yesterday," Hailey added. "Then this morning when I studied Guzmán's journal up close, I noticed the plate was shaped like a sand dollar, and I remembered it looked like the sign for that shop." She bounced a little on her knees. "So Abril took me, and we found a journal *exactly* like Brunilda's, and they do custom engraving, so I had them make one with her initials."

"Then I asked the owner if he knew Guzmán," Abril said. "I described him—very tall, you know? He's pretty memorable—and the owner said yes, he remembers someone like that coming in about a year ago and buying a journal like this."

"So it's not really Brunilda Cano's journal," Hailey finished triumphantly. "Guzmán bought it, and he wrote all the entries. I know that doesn't prove he's faking the séances, but it's something, right? Maybe for some reason he's lying about her being possessed!"

"Maybe he's lying about her even existing," Jamie said, giving me a pointed look.

"No, Guzmán has official records of her," Abril said. "Inés told us. He shared it all with his students—her birth certificate and death certificate, things like that. She saw them."

"Maybe he faked those, too." I sat back against the wall, still gazing at Hailey's journal. "He didn't get them from the library—Jamie and I couldn't find anything about her there. All those books on local history and genealogy, all those records, and there was literally *nothing* about Brunilda Cano in the card catalog. But we found that picture Guzmán has, the one of the convent. The caption says the nun he told us was Brunilda is actually named María Carmen Romero."

"Then we went to the cemetery behind the church," said Jamie. "María was buried there, and lots of other nuns. No Brunilda."

"So . . . so you think Guzmán *invented* her?" Abril's forehead was crinkled. "But why would he do that?"

I slipped my camera back in my pocket. "I don't know, but we need to find Jess and tell her before *P2P* bases an entire episode on the ghost of a person who doesn't even exist."

CHAPTER TWELVE
A DEADLY CASE OF
MiSTAKEN IDENTITY

To: acciopancakes@mymail.net
From: Maytrix@admin.P2P.net
Subject: Just a heads-up

Hi, Kat!

Hope everything's going well in BA. Just wanted to alert you to something that came up on the forums recently, since you haven't logged in for a while. A new user named kbold04 joined and posted some inappropriate stuff in the thread about your blog and . . . well, you, to be honest. Another member alerted me to his post pretty quickly. IMO, the content qualified as harassment, and I deleted it and sent him a warning. Then he posted the same junk again (what a shock, right?). We have a three-strikes policy, so next time he does it, I can just delete his account.

The problem is, if this guy is really persistent, he can just create a new account. We get trolls all the time—usually they give up after a while. Hopefully this one'll just go back under his bridge.

Can't wait for the catacombs episode! I really love *Graveyard Slot*, btw. So glad you and Oscar are on the show.

Maddy (aka Maytrix)

P2P Fan Forum Founder/Admin

PS—jamiebaggins was the member who told me about both posts. Thanks to him, they were barely up for an hour. He's really been looking out for you! ;)

"HEY."

I jumped when I heard Oscar's voice behind me, and I closed my inbox quickly before sliding my phone into my pocket. My heart was still racing from reading Maddy's e-mail. I wasn't sure which was worse: knowing the same person was saying all that horrible stuff about me in the forums, or knowing that Jamie had read it and didn't say anything. Both made me feel the same: angry and ashamed.

"Hey." I scooted over on the sofa as Oscar sat next to me. "Are they still talking about Guzmán upstairs?"

Oscar nodded. Hailey had given Jess the journal a few hours ago, and I'd explained everything we'd learned about Brunilda to the rest of the cast. We were supposed to meet Guzmán and his students for the séance in less than an hour, and they were debating how to handle it: confront him before we started filming, or bust him on camera. If they did it before, he might refuse to even hold the séance, and then pretty much everything else we'd filmed for this episode would be useless. But exposing him while filming was pretty risky, for obvious reasons. Guzmán had a lot at stake—his job, his reputation—and there was no way to predict how he'd react.

"Where are Jamie and Hailey?"

"Video chat with their mom," Oscar replied. "Thiago and Abril went home to tell Inés about the journal. They're coming back tonight while we're filming, though." He kept fidgeting in a nervous sort of way, wiping his palms on his knees, pulling at a loose thread on his shorts.

"Hey, about Thiago," I said. "I'm sorry if I . . . I mean, I was just teasing you about the date thing. I didn't mean to make you mad."

Oscar smiled slightly. "You didn't. Don't worry about it."

"Okay. But for what it's worth . . ." I hesitated, chewing my lip. Oscar fell still, his eyes fixed on the table. "I think maybe he likes you," I blurted out. "So, you know, if you like him, too, you should tell him. That's all."

He was still smiling, but now it looked forced. "Why, because that worked out so well last time I did it?"

"What, with Mark?" I made a face. "Come on, not everyone's that big of a jerk."

"I know that."

"I'm just saying, you can't let what happened with Mark—"

"Stop," Oscar interrupted. "You don't get it. It's not like . . . like *that*." He pointed at the dried-up flower Jamie had given me, which was lying on the table. "I know this stuff is easy for you and that's great, but just . . . don't give me advice, because it's not the same thing. Okay?"

I swallowed hard. "Okay, fine."

"Anyway, I need to talk to you about something else." Oscar shifted a little, still avoiding my gaze. "When the rest of the cast gets down here, I think we have to tell them about Ana."

"Yeah? Why?"

"If we're going to try to get her out of your camera, it

should be a part of the show." I started to respond, but he cut me off. "I know, I know. You hate being on TV, blah blah blah. It's a ghost-hunters show, Kat. You have to tell them about this."

My spine stiffened. "I knew it."

"Knew what?"

"I knew you'd do this," I said, my voice rising a little. "That's why I didn't tell you about seeing Ana in the first place."

Oscar stared at me. "You've *seen* her?"

"At the waterfall, through my camera. And guess what? Before I dropped it into the water, I had pictures of her! *And* pictures of I WANT OUT written all over the cave behind the falls—which she also scratched all over my bathroom a few nights ago, by the way. I even have video of her when I was practicing recording myself so I wouldn't be so freaking nervous about being on camera. Trying to just *get over it*, like someone told me to do."

"What . . . why didn't you tell me?" He sounded more mad than hurt, which just made me even angrier.

"I *wanted* to tell you about it, but I knew you'd do this—force me to tell Jess all about Ana so we'd have to cover it on the show." I was breathing heavily now, tears prickling the corners of my eyes. "Never mind that I didn't even want to be on the stupid show in the first place."

Oscar shook his head in disbelief. "You do realize that this whole catacombs episode might be completely ruined if it turns out Guzmán made Brunilda up, right? This story about Ana is *something,* at least. I can't believe you haven't told anyone just because you don't like being on TV. Your dad's job is at stake here, and my aunt's."

I snorted. "Please, don't pretend that's the reason you want to tell them. This is about you getting more camera time, more *Graveyard Slot* videos, more fans gushing about you and—"

"Oh my God, Kat!" Oscar yelled. "Why are you so mad about that? And who cares what the fans say?"

"Uh, *you*?" A dry laugh escaped my throat. "You love the attention—you're obsessed with reading about yourself on the forums. Probably because it's all lovey-dovey stuff that doesn't make you hate yourself."

Oscar's eyebrows shot up. "Wait, are you talking about that one comment? The one that said you looked like a boy or something?"

"It was more than one," I said defensively. "He's been—"

"So what, a random person you don't even know says a few mean things about you, and suddenly you're too traumatized to be on TV?"

My face burned. "Considering you've been bullied, I kind of thought you'd understand."

"You think a few stupid comments on a video is being bullied?" Oscar rolled his eyes. "Please."

"You know what, Oscar?" I stood up, trembling. But before I could finish the thought—and I wasn't completely sure what the thought was—the elevator doors slid open.

"They're done!" Hailey hurried toward us, followed by Jamie. "Jess said they decided to film the séance, then pull out the journal and confront Guzmán on the show." She danced a little on the spot. "It's going to be dramatic, I bet . . ." Trailing off, she looked from me to Oscar. "Er, is everything okay?"

"Fine," I said shortly, grabbing my camera. "So we're heading to the church?"

"Yeah, Jess said they'd be down here in a few minutes."

"I'll meet you guys there, okay?" Without waiting for a response, I headed to the exit. I couldn't even look at Oscar.

I was crossing the street, hanging the Elapse around my neck, when I heard someone running up behind me. "What's going on?" Jamie asked, panting slightly. "Are you okay?"

"Fantastic," I said. "Thanks for telling me about that jerk in the forums, by the way."

It came out much harsher than I intended, and I forced myself to take a deep breath. I was mad at Oscar, not Jamie.

He stopped on the sidewalk, and I turned to face him. "How'd you find out about the forums?" he asked.

"Maytrix e-mailed me." I rubbed my eyes. "Thank you for reporting it and getting them to delete his posts. I mean it," I added, and Jamie's shoulders relaxed slightly.

"You're welcome. Sorry I didn't tell you earlier." He sounded nervous. "I should've, but . . . I don't know. We were having fun, and I didn't want to upset you."

I waved my hand. "It's fine, really. I've gotten used to his stupid comments." That was a total lie, but hey. Maybe if I faked indifference, I'd feel it eventually.

"Gotten used to them?" Jamie repeated. "I thought you weren't checking the forums."

"Oh..." I started walking again, mentally cursing myself. "Yeah, the same person left a few comments like that on my blog. It's no big deal."

"What?" Jamie's expression darkened. "Did you tell anyone?"

"No."

"Maybe we should—"

"It's fine," I said firmly. "Don't worry about it."

The Elapse bumped against my chest as we walked the rest of the way to the church in silence. Oscar was going to tell the cast about Ana whether I wanted to or not, and I'd told him *everything*. About the messages in the cave and the bathroom. About my embarrassing video. The one with Ana in the mirror.

He'd tell the others, and then they'd realize Ana was possessing *me*, and it all would end up on TV. I couldn't let that happen.

I had to figure out how to exorcise Ana tonight. Alone.

While everyone else was busy running extension cords and setting up equipment, I sneaked off to the sacristy, a small room on the north side of the cathedral. Jess had filmed Dad in here yesterday, since it was one of the places mentioned in Brunilda's fake journal. The sacristy, I'd learned from Dad's segment, was where priests prepared for services and rituals. Fitting, since I had a ritual of my own to perform.

"Okay," I said, walking over to the ornate gold mirror hanging next to a small closet. "Step two: exposure. Come on, Ana. I know it's you."

I stared at my reflection, waiting for . . . what? I had no idea. Red Leer had revealed his identity when I asked Lidia, "Who are you?" and she'd spelled his name on the Ouija board.

Well, this was going to feel really stupid. But what did I have to lose? Squaring my shoulders, I looked my reflection in the eyes.

"Who are you?"

My reflection stared back at me. Then each of us looked down at the camera hanging around the other's neck. Without thinking, I flipped it on and held it up. Now I was watching my reflection through the viewfinder do the same to me.

Only my reflection wasn't alone anymore.

I stared, transfixed, at the dim shape next to me. It was her: the girl from the waterfall, the girl from the video. My eyes flickered back and forth between the screen and the mirror itself. I could only see her through my camera, and she was nothing more than a faint outline, but she was there. She was definitely there.

"Ana?" I whispered.

Slowly, she shook her head.

Not Ana.

Not.

Ana.

That buzzing noise filled my ears again, like a swarm of bees in my head that drowned out everything but the sound of my heart slamming against my ribs. While I should have been surprised, I wasn't. I hadn't been concentrating on Ana when Oscar and I were trying to contact her. And why would she say *I want out* of her own grave, when she was at rest next to her mother, who'd sacrificed so much for her? Sam and Roland had both pointed out that that didn't make sense. Even Jamie admitted it was the one part of his and Oscar's theory that didn't work. But if this girl wasn't Ana, then . . .

"Kat?"

Gasping, I nearly dropped my camera. Hailey stood in the doorway, staring at me with wide eyes.

"Hey!" My voice came out extra squeaky. "I was just, uh, taking pictures! Of, um . . ." I glanced nervously at my reflection, which was alone. "This mirror."

"Oh." Hailey twirled a lock of hair around her finger. "Your dad was looking for you; I think they're almost ready to start. I told him I saw you come back here." She paused. "Are you okay? I thought maybe you were crying or something."

"I'm not crying," I said in surprise. "Why?"

"Well..." Hailey drew a deep breath, and I braced myself for a ramble. "You and Oscar just had a fight in the lobby, obviously, and now he's acting all weird and you're hiding back here. I just thought maybe the fight was about Jamie? Because he likes you and he told Oscar the other night? And Oscar seemed fine with it, but I don't know, then you guys were all yelling at each other in the lobby, and—"

"Hailey," I interjected. "That's not why we were fighting at all, I promise."

"Oh." She gave me a shrewd look. "So this isn't one of those stupid love-triangle situations? Where you're, like, all *torn* between two boys or whatever? Because I hate when that happens in movies and stuff."

Despite everything, I couldn't help giggling. "No. I like your brother."

Closing her eyes, Hailey tilted her head back and whispered: "*Ew.*" Then, shaking herself, she smiled at me. "Okay! So what happened with Oscar?"

"He was being a jerk, that's what. Nothing new." I felt a flash of guilt for saying it, but I was still too hurt to care.

"You guys argue a lot," Hailey said thoughtfully. "Usually about little stuff, though. I've never seen you look that mad at each other."

"Yeah." I adjusted my camera strap, glancing in the mirror one more time before heading to the door. "Maybe we're just not cut out to be friends."

Her eyes widened. "Don't say that!"

I shrugged, my stomach twisting again. "Why not?"

"Because . . ." Hailey scrunched her nose. "Well, because you guys are like me and Jamie."

"Ha." I walked past her out of the sacristy, and she hurried to keep up at my side. "Trust me, Hailey. It's not like that at all."

"Okay, well . . ." Hailey grabbed my arm, stopping me before we reached the pews. Her bright blue eyes were very serious. "When someone annoys you so much you want to scream, but you love him anyway because you can't help it? That's what it's like having a brother. Just so you know."

With that, she headed to the back of the church, leaving me feeling more guilty and frustrated than ever. I could see Oscar waiting by the entrance to the courtyard talking to Mi Jin. The rest of the cast was listening to Professor Guzmán prattle away excitedly near the altar. Inés and a few other students stood not far from them, and I couldn't help noticing the way Inés kept shooting glares in Guzmán's direction. Dad waved at me before slinging a cable coil over his shoulder.

"Ready to head down there, Kat?"

"Coming." Adjusting my camera strap one more time, I took a deep breath. Time to get this fake séance over with.

THE catacombs had been warm when we entered, but after a few minutes crammed with over a dozen people, the air was hot and stifling. The atmosphere was tense, too. Guzmán's students sat around the table, whispering among themselves, while Inés glowered silently. Jess was filming Guzmán, who stood in front of one of the skull circles, talking cheerfully and holding up the fake journal. I started heading over to where Dad was talking to Lidia, but Mi Jin stopped me.

"Stand over there next to Oscar," she said distractedly, adjusting the mic on top of her camera. "We don't have enough footage of you two for this episode so far. I'm supposed to get some before we start." She glanced up when I groaned. "What's wrong?"

"Nothing." I stalked over to where Oscar was leaning against the wall, Mi Jin right behind me. Her camera's red light flickered on, and every muscle in my body tensed.

"So, guys," Mi Jin said brightly. "On the latest *Graveyard Slot* video, you tried contacting Brunilda, but ended up getting what looked like it might be the same message you got back in Salvador. A few minutes ago, Oscar filled me in on a pretty interesting theory."

I closed my eyes. He'd already done it. Of *course* he had. The traitor.

"Yeah, I think Ana Arias followed us," Oscar said shortly. He wasn't using his usual cheesy reporter voice; he sounded angry. "It's the only thing that makes sense. Right, Kat?"

He stared at me pointedly. I focused on a spot above Mi Jin's head, fists clenched at my sides. "Actually, no," I said. "It's not."

Mi Jin smiled encouragingly. "Then why do you think you got the same message?"

"Because we faked it."

Her eyebrow ring shot up, the smile vanishing from her face. "What?"

"Yeah, we faked it." I turned to face Oscar, whose mouth was open. "Right?"

The red light went off. "Did you really?" Mi Jin asked softly, lowering her camera. Her disappointed expression was almost enough to make me tell the truth.

"No!" Oscar sputtered, still staring at me. "What are you doing? You said you saw Ana at the waterfall, and—"

I shrugged. "I lied. I made it all up, just like Guzmán did. Guess it'll fit with the theme of this episode, huh?" With that, I walked over to where Roland leaned against the wall, watching everyone at the table. A few seconds later, Oscar appeared at my side.

"Why did you do that?" he said in a loud whisper. "They won't use it on the show!"

I smiled humorlessly. "Aw, what a shame."

Oscar's eyes were bugging out. "Kat, did you just—are you seriously pretending you made up all that stuff about Ana just so you won't be on TV for a few extra minutes?"

"I'm not pretending," I said to my feet. "It was all a lie."

Roland was looking at us curiously. "Ana?"

"Yup." My voice rose a little. "I lied about seeing her. Sorry."

I kept my eyes fixed on the floor, willing them to start the séance so I wouldn't have to answer any more questions. I was a terrible liar, but it didn't matter. No one could prove I *hadn't* lied, and now they wouldn't use any of the Ana stuff on TV. Take that, Oscar.

"Everyone, thank you so much for being here," Guzmán said grandly, spreading his arms in a welcoming gesture. The hum of chatter died down. Jess and Mi Jin were slowly circling the table, their cameras trained on the professor. He seemed relaxed and happy, totally oblivious to the tense expressions and shifty glances going on around him. "The last year has been extraordinary, to say the least. When my students and I first gathered together down here to contact Brunilda, I never dreamed we'd get the results we have since received. Tonight, you will see—and record—proof that paranormal activity is real."

I didn't dare make eye contact with anyone else. I almost

felt sorry for Professor Guzmán, who clearly had no idea the whole cast was onto his lies.

"We typically begin our séances with a reading from Brunilda's journal," Guzmán went on. "Ms. Bettencourt, seeing as the experience of possession is something you have in common with Brunilda, I was wondering if you might do the honors?"

He handed her a sheet of paper, which Lidia accepted with a tight smile. Jess knelt at her side for a close-up, while Mi Jin continued prowling the small room, filming everyone's reactions as Lidia read.

"Today when I dipped my fingers into the holy water, it burned like acid. But though it felt as if my skin were melting off the bone, my hand was unblemished."

I did my best to ignore Mi Jin's camera and focus on my own. Who was the ghost I kept seeing through the viewfinder? I had to make her reveal her identity.

"My fellow sisters were watching, so I gritted my teeth and touched the water again, then anointed my face as they had done, thinking perhaps this would drive away the evil taking residence inside me."

Maybe I should just dunk my camera in holy water, I thought wryly. A nagging sensation started in the back of my mind, like I'd forgotten something important. Something about water. The waterfall? No, the pool, the first time I'd seen the ghost. I tried to focus, picturing everything about that moment. The way she'd looked at me, waved at me. I couldn't see a single feature, but somehow I'd just known she was a girl.

"Throughout the service, I struggled not to scream or cry from the pain, certain that by the end my grinning skull would be exposed."

And then I'd dropped my camera in the water.

"Then everyone would see me for what I truly am now. They would see the monster."

The buzzing noise returned full force, and I squeezed my eyes closed, willing it to stop. A few seconds later I could barely make out Lidia's words.

"But a peek in the mirror revealed my looks had not changed. I wish I could say the same for my soul."

For a split second, the world went silent. My head felt like it was gripped in a vise, the pressure so intense I couldn't even scream. Then it released, and I gasped for air, leaning heavily against the bones. There was a shout and a crash, but my vision was too blurred to see what was going on.

The room was loud now, everyone talking at once, chairs scraping back. When I blinked and squinted, I half expected to see them all crowded around me. But when things came back into focus, I saw they were all surrounding Mi Jin, who had dropped her camera. Jess was still filming as Lidia helped Mi Jin inspect her equipment for damage.

"It just . . . it was like someone knocked it out of my hands," Mi Jin was saying, her voice shaking a little.

Guzmán smiled. "Brunilda is with us," he said. "Back to your seats, please." His students sat quickly, their expressions ranging from excited to nervous. Dad eyed Guzmán with suspicion as he returned to his chair.

A light pulsation on my chest caught my attention, and I looked down to see my Elapse turning off and on, lens extending and retracting over and over. I pressed the power button a few times, but it wouldn't stop. Oscar watched me, but didn't say anything.

"It's rolling," Mi Jin said, the red light on her camera blinking back on. I gripped my Elapse, worried that the light mechanical whirring would disrupt the séance. But no one seemed to notice.

"Brunilda Cano . . ." Guzmán's voice was soft, almost hypnotic. His students all wore intense expressions of concentration, except for Inés, whose face was growing steadily redder. "Welcome back. We'd like to talk to you about your exorcism."

The room was still. I stared down into my camera lens, watching it open and close like a blinking eye, catching my reflection every other second. *Who are you?*

A sliver of an idea crept into my mind, like that first thin line of brightness on the horizon at sunrise, but it slid out of sight before I could fully grasp it. Guzmán was still talking, his words nothing more than a drone. Because it was here. I could feel it. The monster, whatever it was, the one I'd sensed at the willow tree. It was in this room.

Someone cried out in shock. I watched in a detached sort of way as the table, the entire table, rose up off the ground an inch, two inches. For a few seconds, everyone froze. Then the table fell with a heavy *thud,* and chaos erupted.

Inés shot to her feet, rapidly screaming at Guzmán in Spanish. The other students looked shocked at first, though it wasn't long before understanding dawned on their faces as they listened to her rant. Turning to Lidia, Inés clenched her fists at her side. "Show him the journal," she pleaded. "Please."

Lidia exchanged a glance with Dad before slowly pulling the journal from her bag and holding it up for the others to see. "We got this from a shop in Plaza Dorrego," she explained, flipping through the blank pages for Jess's camera. "Identical to yours. And we have proof that the woman you claim is Brunilda in that photo is actually Sister María Carmen Romero."

"There are no records of a nun by the name of Brunilda Cano at this church," Dad added somberly. "Would you care to explain, Professor?"

The room fell absolutely silent. It was as if we were all collectively holding our breaths, staring at Guzmán and waiting. He clasped his hands, exhaled slowly, and smiled.

"Yes. I created Brunilda Cano. She never existed."

Inés sat down heavily in her chair, glowering. But two of his other students began yelling like she had, while a third stomped out of the room. Jess and Mi Jin were doing their best to capture all the reactions; Lidia and Dad looked disappointed but unsurprised, and Guzmán seemed weirdly calm, even pleased. Sam was running his hands under the table, brow knitted. He turned in our direction with a questioning look. I glanced up and saw Roland was smiling.

"What?" Oscar asked. "Why are you so happy?"

"Because Guzmán's experiment worked. It's brilliant."

"What? He *made her up*. She doesn't exist."

"He made her up," Roland agreed. "But she exists."

Oscar looked as bewildered as I felt. "That doesn't make sense."

Sticking his hands in his pockets, Roland surveyed the unfolding chaos as Guzmán attempted to calm his angry students. "The table levitated," he said, apparently enjoying himself now. "A force knocked Mi Jin's camera from her hands. The temperature dropped. Brunilda might be fake, but the paranormal activity? That was real."

I couldn't process what he was saying. Oscar kept asking questions, but all the talking and yelling blurred into a dull noise. Someone was looking at me. Someone standing on the staircase. I turned slowly and saw the shape of her in the shadows. She beckoned for me to follow and I did, slipping out before anyone could see, my camera still pulsing on-off, on-off against my chest.

CHAPTER FOURTEEN
THE OTHER DAUGHTER . . .
NOW IN 3-D!

SHE stuck to the side of the church, creeping against the stained glass–covered wall like a shadow. I followed her at a crouch. Guzmán's student, the one who had walked out in anger moments before I did, was talking to Abril and Thiago—describing all the drama downstairs, I assumed. Abril was translating everything he said for Jamie and Hailey, who must have been waiting in the church for us to finish filming. None of them saw us, two girls slipping behind the columns, around the last pew, and out the doors.

It was harder to see her outside now that the sun had set. But that didn't matter, because I knew where she was going. My camera continued whirring on and off as I hurried into the park and down the dirt path, occasionally tripping over a root in my haste. I'd lost sight of her completely—until the willow tree came into view.

She stood across the clearing, and I slowed to a halt. Slowly lifting her arm, she waved at me, just as she had back at the waterfall. Then she vanished.

I broke into a run, camera thumping against my chest. The thin, delicate hanging leaves grazed the top of my head as I circled the willow, slipping over the smooth gray rocks piled around the roots. I had to see her face. I had to know who she was.

Finally, I stopped, hands on my knees as I struggled to catch my breath. Something on the bark caught my eye. A message, crudely carved into the trunk.

I GOT OUT

My camera was still turning on and off, so I pulled my phone out of my pocket and snapped a picture. Stepping closer, I touched the letters one at a time, tracing them, feeling each deep, angry scratch. A sliver of wood slit the tip of my finger, and I winced. The Elapse fell silent as the lens retracted and the power light turned off. The world tilted. I leaned my head against the tree and closed my eyes briefly.

"What are you doing?"

Gasping, I spun around to find Oscar standing a few feet away. His gaze moved from my bleeding finger to the trunk, and his eyes widened.

"Is that . . ." He stepped closer. "Did you do that?"

"You can see it?" My voice broke with relief. This wasn't

like in the bathroom or the cave. This wasn't a hallucination.

Oscar was giving me a weird look. "Why wouldn't I be able to see it?"

"Because, I . . ." I shook my head, touching the trunk again. "I thought maybe I was seeing things. And no, I didn't do it."

"It looked like you were."

"No, I was just touching it." I glanced around the clearing, wiping the blood from my finger on the hem of my shirt. "Did you come by yourself?"

"Yeah."

"You left while they were still filming? Aren't you worried about letting down all your fans?"

It was mean, and I felt rotten as soon as I said it. But the ghost was still there; I just knew it. And I had a feeling she wasn't going to reveal her identity in front of Oscar. I needed him to leave.

He was silent for a few seconds. "Just because being on TV freaks you out doesn't mean it's wrong that I like it," he said, and I rolled my eyes.

"You *love* it."

Oscar's eyes flashed with anger. "You know, I followed you because you looked like you were about to have some sort of meltdown back there and I wanted to make sure you were okay. Sorry I bothered. So what if I like doing interviews? And reading about myself on the forums?" His voice was getting all high and shaky. "Because you're right, Kat. I *do* like that they like me. It feels really good after everything else that's happened, between my best friend deciding he hates me and making every single day at school completely miserable, and me getting expelled thanks to those stupid notes in my locker, and then my dad . . ." Oscar stared at the tree behind me, his eyes suddenly red and shiny. "He knew, Kat. He already knew that I liked Mark because it turns out my aunt told him months ago. He never brought it up, and he blew me off when I tried to talk to him about it over Thanksgiving. He told me I'm just going through a *phase* and I'd get over it, and then he shut down and wouldn't listen to anything else I said because apparently just talking about it weirds him out so much he can't even look at me, and . . ."

Then I couldn't understand any more because Oscar was crying, *really* crying, and before I could say anything he sat down on one of the roots and buried his face in his hands.

"Oscar?" My voice cracked a little, and I tentatively sat down next to him. My stomach churned with guilt. "I didn't know . . . I shouldn't have . . . I'm so sorry. I didn't mean any of that stuff I said before."

He let out a little laugh. "Yeah, you did. It's fine. You're right; I've been obsessed with all this TV stuff. I didn't ask Aunt Lidia about that interview because I thought she might say no and I really wanted to do it. Same thing with the web series. I knew you wouldn't want to do it, so . . ." Wiping his face with his sleeve, Oscar shook his head. "I'm sorry."

"It's okay." I suddenly realized my cheeks were wet, too. We sat quietly for a minute, carefully looking anywhere but at each other. "What did you mean about getting expelled because of some notes in your locker?" I said at last, just to break the silence. "I thought it was because you got into a fight with Mark."

Oscar sighed. "Yeah, and the fight was because of the notes. He and some other kids printed out, like, hundreds of pages with a bunch of . . . stuff typed on it."

"Stuff?"

"About me," he said, and my heart sank. "Words. Jokes. You know. All printed in a giant font you could pretty much see from space. Then they stuffed them all in my locker so when I got to school that morning and opened it, the notes came falling out in front of everyone."

I let out a long, slow breath. "That's . . . horrible."

"Yeah. The stupid thing is, I kept them."

I looked at him sharply. "You what?"

"I stuffed them all in my gym bag, brought them home, and kept them under my bed." Oscar sounded almost amused. "Isn't that dumb? And I *read* them. Like, a lot." I just stared at him, unable to respond. "They kept doing it, too, because I never showed a teacher or anyone. I didn't want people seeing that stuff. So they knew it was getting to me, but they knew they weren't going to get in trouble, either, because I was too . . . because I wouldn't rat them out. But I was getting angrier and angrier, and one day I was done with it, I guess. I went and found Mark after lunch, and I wasn't really thinking. I just went up to him and . . .

punched him. Broke his nose."

He glanced at me nervously. When I didn't say anything, he continued.

"A teacher broke it up before he could hit me back. I had to talk to everyone—the principal, counselor—and they kept asking why I did it. But, you know, I didn't want to tell them about everything. So I got expelled and Mark didn't."

"Oscar . . ."

"I know, the notes," Oscar interrupted. His words were spilling out faster now, a fresh tear slipping down his cheek. "My aunt found them, like, a month later. She was *furious*, because I had proof Mark had provoked me and I never showed the principal. Not that it was an excuse for hitting him, but at least they'd know the reason. She was even angrier when she realized I kept them because I still read them."

"Why?" My voice cracked on the question. Probably because I knew the answer. But I wanted to hear him explain it. "Why were you still reading them?"

Oscar picked up a stick and started digging a small hole in the dirt. "I don't know. My aunt told me when someone says the worst things we think about ourselves, we start thinking that means it's all true. And . . . I guess that's right. Because the stuff in those notes, they made me hate Mark . . . but they made me hate myself even more." The stick snapped in two, and he tossed it onto the grass. "I couldn't stop reading them because they made me think I was right to hate myself. Doesn't make any sense, I know."

"Um . . ." I wiped my eyes before pulling my phone out of my pocket. "Actually, I . . ." Pressing my lips together, I opened my photo album and found the first kbold04 screenshot. Hesitantly, I handed it to Oscar.

He squinted at the screen. "What's . . . wait, this is that comment you told me about?"

"That's the second one," I said. "I deleted it. There's more, though."

Oscar started swiping, pausing to read each screenshot. "How many are there?"

Fifty-three. "Um . . . around fifty, I think."

"Did you show your dad?"

I snorted. "My blog still exists, doesn't it? Obviously I didn't tell him."

"Maybe you should, though." Oscar paused on one of the most vulgar comments, his mouth dropping open.

"He never makes threats or anything," I said quickly. "It's not like—like the letters Emily sent Sam."

"So? That doesn't make this okay." Oscar flipped to the next screenshot, his expression growing increasingly darker. Then he turned to face me. "Wait, you don't believe what he's saying, do you?"

"You believed your notes." I blinked as my eyes filled with tears again.

"Yeah, and my aunt made me throw them away because they were garbage," Oscar said firmly. "So are these comments. None of this is true, Kat. I'm deleting them, okay?"

I nodded, because I didn't trust myself to speak. I stared down at my feet as Oscar went through the whole album, tapping with a bit more force than was necessary. When he finished, he practically shoved my phone back at me.

"Thanks." I took it, frowning. "Are you mad at me?"

"No." Oscar paused. "Okay, maybe a little. Mostly I'm mad at whoever that idiot is. And at myself. If I'd known about..." He gestured at the screen, brow furrowed. "I mean, no wonder you were acting so weird about *Graveyard Slot*, if that person kept leaving comments like that. I'm really sorry I—"

"You didn't know," I said. "Don't worry about it."

"Okay." He glanced at me. "Will you tell me if you get more?"

"Yeah."

Hesitating, I held my hand out, palm up. Oscar took it, interlacing our fingers, and I ignored the faint throbbing of the cut I'd gotten from the tree. "We should probably get back," I said. "Do you think anyone's even noticed we're missing yet?"

"Probably not." He clasped my hand tightly as we headed across the clearing. "It was getting pretty chaotic down there. Hey, why'd you come out to the tree, anyway?"

"Chasing a ghost," I said lightly. "What else?"

Oscar raised an eyebrow. "Seriously? Wait, was it Ana?"

"Nope." I told him everything that had happened,

starting with the mirror girl in the sacristy. "And that message on the tree, you saw it. *I got out.* So if she was in my camera, whoever she is, she's not there anymore."

"But if it's not Ana, who is it?"

"I don't know," I admitted. It bothered me more than I wanted to let on to Oscar. I'd been so close to finally discovering her identity before he showed up. But it was okay. I had the feeling she was ready for me to know now. I'd get another chance soon, and I wasn't afraid anymore.

"Oh," I said. "I did figure something out down in the catacombs. Check this out." I flipped the Elapse on and held it up. Oscar kept glancing at it as we continued walking down the path.

"Well?"

"Just wait."

After a few seconds, he stopped. "Okay, what are you doing? This is . . ." He looked around. "Hang on . . . Are we even going the right way?"

My hands were sweating and my heart was hammering away, but I couldn't help smiling. "Yeah. Look." I flipped the camera off. My pulse slowed immediately, and I saw Oscar's shoulders relax. "It makes us feel anxious. And *lost.*"

Oscar frowned. "So it's still possessed?"

"Think about that feeling," I said. "It's how we all felt at the waterfall. Nervous, panicky, lost. Like the hikers, right? Because it's a residual haunting. All their emotions were trapped there."

"Right . . ."

"Trapped in the rocks, in the trees, in the *water.*"

I lifted my camera strap, letting the Elapse dangle like a hypnotist's necklace. Oscar's mouth fell open.

"You dropped it into the water, and—"

"It soaked up the residual emotions," I finished. "That's what I think."

"Wow." We reached the park exit and picked up our pace as the church entrance came into view. "So you can't use your camera anymore without having a panic attack? That kind of sucks."

"Yeah," I agreed. But something else had just occurred to me. According to what Jamie and I had read, I shouldn't have been able to exorcise the ghost without knowing her identity. But according to her message on the tree, she "got out."

That sliver of an idea was back, so thin and fragile, I couldn't quite grasp it fully. "Did you understand what Roland was saying about Brunilda?" I asked Oscar.

"Just that Guzmán made her up, but he wasn't faking the other stuff, like with the table. I don't really get it."

"Me either," I said. "Let's find out."

The crew had moved from the catacombs into the church, equipment spread out between the altar and the first row of pews. The mood had changed entirely since I'd left; now it was all smiles and excited chatter. Even Inés and

Guzmán's other students looked thrilled as they watched Dad interview their professor.

Oscar and I snuck up to the front, keeping behind the columns. It didn't look like anyone had noticed we were missing yet. Well, none of the adults. Jamie kept glancing around, and he spotted us almost right away. He nudged Hailey, whose face lit up when she saw us. They left Abril and Thiago, who were watching as Inés joined the interview, and hurried over.

"Where'd you guys go?" Jamie whispered.

"The willow tree," I said, and quickly explained about the girl who'd appeared in the catacombs. "But it's not Ana," I added. "I don't know who she is."

Hailey's eyes were shining. "It's Brunilda, I bet," she said. "It totally makes sense now."

"What? No, she—"

"No, listen," Hailey went on. "That was the whole point of Guzmán's experiment. He said he wanted to prove that— what did he say exactly?"

"That paranormal activity is a manifestation of the mind, which makes it real," Jamie said. "He needed his students to believe Brunilda existed for it to work. They did, and because they believed in her, they got actual results. The stuff that happened during his séances, like the table floating and all that, he wasn't faking any of it!"

"So they *did* conjure Brunilda down there," Hailey finished. "And she led you to the willow tree! Ah, I wish someone had gone with you to film it. Are you going to tell

Jess about the message? She'll probably want to get—"

"No," I interrupted. "No . . . it can't be Brunilda. I saw this ghost at the waterfall, before we even got here."

Hailey asked. "Are you sure it's the same one?"

"Yes. It's not Brunilda." Ignoring the glance Jamie and Oscar exchanged, I looked around the church until I spotted Roland. "I'll be right back, okay?"

I hurried off without waiting for a response. Roland was sitting in the third row, flipping through Brunilda's journal. I slid into the pew behind him and tapped his shoulder.

"How can Brunilda be a made-up person but a real ghost?" I had to struggle to keep my voice down. "That doesn't make sense."

Roland looked at me curiously. "Have you been crying? Your eyes are all red."

"What? No." Instinctively, I wiped my eyes even though they were dry. "Look, that ghost at the waterfall I told you about, the one I thought was Ana Arias? She's . . . it's not Ana, but I'm still seeing her. And you said that was my brain *tricking* me." I felt slightly panicky, so I glanced down to make sure my camera was still off. "Is that what this Brunilda thing is? She didn't exist, but Guzmán tricked us into believing she's real, and suddenly somehow she is? I don't get it."

Setting the journal down, Roland grabbed his backpack and started rummaging inside. "I think I can explain it," he said. "So the town I grew up in had one library. Really small, really old. When I was five, my brother told me it was haunted. Aha, here they are." He pulled out a wad of napkins and handed them to me. "They're clean, I swear."

"Thanks." I took one and blew my nose.

"My brother said that the library was haunted by its very first librarian," Roland continued. "She was killed when someone knocked over a shelf, which knocked over another shelf—domino effect kind of thing—and, anyway, she was crushed to death. Her name was Ellie."

I started to say something, then thought better of it. Roland had gotten so close-lipped when Sam mentioned Ellie back at the waterfall, and I wanted to hear the rest of the story.

"My brother told me her ghost was spotted every year at midnight on the anniversary of her death," he went on. "He had all kinds of other stories about her, too. Like how people sometimes felt cold standing near the shelf that crushed her, or felt her breath on their necks if they shelved a book in the wrong place. I was pretty obsessed with the whole idea, and I spent a ton of time at the library hoping to have some sort of sighting. But I knew if I wanted to see Ellie, it had to be on the day she died. So when I was nine years old, that's what I did."

"At midnight, though?" I couldn't help but ask. "Wasn't the library closed?"

"Yup. I squeezed myself between the card catalog and the wall a few minutes before the library closed and waited until everyone was gone and it was locked up. Then, camped out at her shelf, I waited. Sure enough, right at midnight, there she was."

My eyes widened. "You really saw her?"

Roland nodded. "Barely, but yes. She disappeared after maybe a minute, but I saw her. I definitely saw her." He smiled and shook his head. "My mom grounded me for about a month, but I thought it was worth it. Until my brother came home that weekend—he was in college by then—and I told him about what I'd done, that I'd seen Ellie. He just started cracking up. Wanna guess why?"

He lifted Brunilda's journal, and I frowned. "I don't . . . oh. *Oh*."

"Yep," Roland said cheerfully. "There was no Ellie. No librarian had ever been crushed by a shelf of books. Just a dumb story he'd made up to scare his little brother. He had no idea I'd been obsessing over it for years. It was the family joke till I graduated high school." He tossed the journal back on the pew. "After a while, I just went along with it. Went to prom alone and told everyone Ellie was my date, that sort of thing. The older I got, the more I wondered if maybe I *had* just imagined her. But a part of me still insisted she was real. It wasn't until I got to college that I started to figure it out."

"Why, what happened?"

"I met Sam," Roland said simply. "Weirdo guy in my psych class who thought he could talk to dead people. I ended up telling him the whole story about Ellie. He said it was just like when he'd contact a dead person for some stranger and get a 'message from the beyond' that he couldn't possibly know; he received it because the person *believed* in what he was doing, and so they got the message they wanted. Sam said not believing is just as powerful as believing, and if I believed in Ellie, then maybe she was real after all. And I . . ." He paused, grinning. "Thought he was nuts. But I also sort of understood what he was saying. That's when I got into parapsychology."

I sighed. "But the point is, your brain tricked you into seeing things. You saw Ellie, but she still wasn't *real.*"

"No?" Roland arched an eyebrow. "Then why did Guzmán and the rest of us see that table float? We didn't believe in Brunilda, but his students did. *Their* belief made her ghost real, and *we* saw proof."

I sat back against the pew, frowning. It was starting to make sense now. All of it.

Roland was still watching me, brow knitted. "Kat."

"What?"

"You're crying."

Startled, I touched my cheek, then wiped my face with the napkins. "Ugh, sorry."

"What's going on?"

"Nothing. Girl stuff, you don't want to hear about it." Ignoring the skeptical look he gave me, I shoved the napkins into my pocket. "Looks like they're finishing up." I pointed at Jess, who was shaking Guzmán's hand, camera hanging at her side. Roland glanced over, too, and I slipped out of the pew and down the aisle before he could ask me anything else.

"Mind if I jump in the shower first?" Dad asked as soon as we got back to our hotel room.

"Sure." I flopped back on the bed and pulled my phone out of my pocket. Whistling cheerfully, Dad grabbed his pajamas and headed into the bathroom. The whole cast was clearly thrilled about how things had turned out with Guzmán. I'd spent the last hour pretending to smile and act just as excited. But I wasn't.

I opened my inbox first, keeping my right finger off the screen. The cut wasn't bleeding anymore, but it still stung.

From: invitation@justbridalstuff.com
To: acciopancakes@mymail.net
Subject: Monica Has Invited YOU to a Bridal Shower!
For: Katya Sinclair

WILL ATTEND　　　　　　　**WILL NOT ATTEND**

Please join us for a bridal shower in honor of
MONICA MILLS
Sunday, March 1, at 6:00 p.m.
Maison Bellerose, Chelsea, Ohio
Hosted by Edie Mills

I closed the e-mail quickly and opened my blog

dashboard. No new comments.

Sighing, I tossed my phone on the comforter, then pulled off the Elapse, too. I wouldn't be able to put off telling Mom I didn't want to be in her wedding much longer. I should just call her before we left for New York the next day and get it over with. The thought made my stomach turn over.

I rolled onto my side and winced as something sharp dug into my thigh. Sitting up, I ran my hands over the comforter, then stuck my hand in my pocket. And pulled out a rock.

I stared at it, bewildered. It was about half the size of my palm, and flat, with one side tapered to a razor-sharp point. Smooth, dark gray with a marbled pattern . . . like the rocks under the willow tree. When had I put this in my pocket?

Unsettled, I stood up and walked over to the desk to examine the rock under the lamp. I remembered playing with one of these when we were filming the séance under the tree. But I hadn't even been wearing these shorts. And I didn't remember that rock having such a sharp edge. Sharp enough to carve words into tree bark. Oscar had said it looked like that's what I was doing tonight. But I hadn't.

Had I?

A sudden movement in the mirror made the blood in my veins freeze.

I carefully set the rock down on the desk, keeping my eyes averted. But I could see her in my peripheral vision: the girl standing next to me in the mirror. Not transparent anymore—just as solid, just as *real* as me. And I knew who she was before I even looked up at her face. I'd known ever since she appeared in the catacombs, but I wouldn't let myself believe it because I didn't see how it was possible. But now I understood. Guzmán had created Brunilda. Roland had created Ellie.

And I'd created the Thing.

CHAPTER FIFTEEN
IT'S BAAAAACK!

New comments (1)
Anonymous: I GOT OUT

IT-SHE—wore a dress, lacy and delicate. She had my old braid, the one I'd chopped off before leaving Chelsea, hanging over her shoulder. A few loose tendrils curled around her face, and long lashes framed her cold, expressionless eyes.

Then she smiled. Or sneered. I couldn't tell which, but it was enough to break me out of my trance. I stumbled away, staring at the space next to me. Frantically, I searched the room: the closet, under the beds, the ceiling (because I'd seen enough horror movies to know people never think to look *up* until it's too late).

I was alone. When I forced myself to look back in the mirror, all I saw was my frightened reflection, alone.

"Bathroom's all yours!" I jumped at the sound of Dad's voice, banging my knee against the desk. He raised an eyebrow as he crossed the room and pulled back the blankets on his bed. "You okay?"

"Yeah! Fine." My voice came out all squeaky. "You just startled me."

Dad laughed. "Hours underground in a room made out of human bones, and you get scared by your old man coming out of the bathroom."

I forced myself to smile, even though my insides were still shivering.

An hour later, Dad was snoring away. The lights were off, but the TV was blaring. I was lying in bed, doing my best not to glance at the mirror every few seconds. I wasn't sure how I'd ever sleep again.

The Thing had been real to me pretty much all my life. But this was different. Just like Brunilda, now she was real to everyone else. She'd knocked Mi Jin's camera out of her hands in the catacombs. She'd left a message on the willow tree, and Oscar had seen it. She wasn't just in my head anymore. She was *out.*

What was she going to do next?

From: timelord2002@mymail.net
To: acciopancakes@mymail.net, trishhhhbequiet@mymail.net
Subject: Re: hey!

Sorry you hate being on TV. The *Graveyard Slot* thing is really cool, though. How did things turn out with the professor making up that ghost? Do you think the episode will be okay?

My mom did indeed make peppermint brownies. Come back to Chelsea and you can have all you want. :)
Mark

From: trishhhhbequiet@mymail.net
To: acciopancakes@mymail.net, timelord2002@mymail.net
Subject: Re: Re: hey!

well hello there, MS. TV STAR! :D i'm leaving for florida tomorrow, coming back after new year's. how long will you be in new york?

i looked up that rumorz interview you mentioned—oscar's really funny. are you going to do any interviews? you should!!

Ideas on How to Get Out of the Wedding from Hell:

1. your spider-web dress idea
2. you and i are co-bridesmaids and we walk down the aisle holding hands, dressed like those evil sisters from *The Monster in Her Closet*
3. you replace whatever music your mom picked with the soundtrack from *Cannibal Clown Circus* (still haven't forgiven you for making me watch that one btw)
4. when it's your turn to walk down the aisle, mark sets fang loose (sidenote: is it possible to train a snake to be a ring bearer? must research)
5. YOU TELL YOUR MOM YOU DON'T WANT TO GO. seriously, kat. you don't want to do it, so tell her. and if she's hurt, well, whatever. i've seen her hurt your feelings a million times. just tell her.

<3<3<3 trish

When our alarm went off at 8:00 a.m., I rolled over and flipped it off before Dad had even budged. My eyes were sore and scratchy, and my head felt like it was suddenly too heavy for my neck, but I was relieved. Every time I'd started drifting off, I'd seen that other version of my face in the mirror and jerked awake again, terrified.

But the Thing didn't make an appearance as I brushed my teeth and attempted to brush the knots out of my hair. I changed into shorts and my *Zombies Are People, Too!* shirt—appropriate, considering my appearance this morning—and left the bathroom quickly.

The rest of the cast looked pretty zombie-like, too, although probably not because they'd lain awake all night, wondering if they'd really created an alternate ghost version of themselves. Professor Guzmán and some of his students had come to see us off. Outside, I could see Inés and Abril chatting animatedly with Mi Jin while helping her load luggage into the back of one of our rental vans, while Roland and Sam were deep in discussion with Guzmán. Dad joined Jess and Lidia, who were going over our itinerary with Mr. Cooper by the checkout desk.

Jamie waved from where he was standing with Hailey, Oscar, and Thiago near the entrance. I dragged my suitcase over, doing my best impression of a normal, fully-awake girl who was not on the verge of a complete meltdown.

"Hello," I said, smiling at Thiago before pointing at the croissant in Hailey's hand. "That. I need one of those. Or, like, three."

"I'll go with you," Jamie said immediately, and we headed into the breakfast room. I grabbed a handful of napkins and studied the selection of pastries. Jamie pointed to the smaller croissants in the middle of the tray. "Those are chocolate."

"Done." I took three, along with a blueberry muffin for the plane.

"So you've never been to New York, right?" Jamie asked.

"Nope," I said, filling a cup with orange juice. "Dad and I didn't even pack winter clothes. I think my grandma's going to send some."

"Well, there's this supernatural museum I've been to a few times, and right now they've got a psychic photography exhibit, and—"

"A *what*?" I interrupted, suddenly much more awake.

Jamie grinned. "Physic photography. It's when the image in a photo appears through telepathy, not because it was actually there when the picture was taken. Supposedly it's even possible with video."

"Wait, you mean, like, someone projects the image onto the photo with their thoughts?"

"Yup."

My mind started racing. The video I'd taken on my Elapse, when the Thing had appeared like a shadow in the mirror . . . when I'd seen her through the viewfinder across the pool and in the sacristy . . .

"Hailey's the one who found out about the exhibit," Jamie was saying. "So she got our mom to e-mail the director a few days ago, and she ended up arranging a private demonstration for us with the photographer on Saturday.

And, um . . . do you want to go?"

"Um, *yeah*," I said fervently. "That's a great idea for the web series! Hailey's really good at this; I should ask if she wants to help me research for some of my other posts."

"Oh." Jamie's eyes widened. "Um. Actually, I meant . . . do you want to go with me? As, like, a second date kind of thing."

He sounded nervous, and for a few seconds I managed to forget about ghosts and photos. "*Yes*. Yes, I definitely want to do that."

Jamie beamed. "Okay! Just to be clear, Hailey isn't actually going with us."

"Got it," I said, trying not to laugh. "Your sister doesn't go on your dates, she just plans them."

"Yeah, she's obsessed with the whole matchmaking thing. She wasn't joking about Natalie Blackwell, either," Jamie added, lowering his voice. "You might want to warn Oscar."

"Natalie?" I frowned. "Oh, that girl who came to your viewing party?"

"Yeah." Jamie shrugged. "She's nice and all. But Hailey's not always good at this. Natalie might not be his type." It might have been my imagination, but I thought I saw him glance briefly at Thiago.

I'd meant it when I told Oscar that I suspected Thiago might like him. Had Jamie noticed, too? I couldn't ask him, obviously. After everything Oscar had confided in me last night about Mark, I didn't want to give him any more unwanted advice. But we were leaving for the airport in a few minutes. If Oscar *had* decided to talk to Thiago, I could at least make it a little easier. After all, he'd gone along with Hailey's plan to send Jamie and me on a date.

Mr. Cooper was just heading outside with Dad and Jess, while Roland and Sam were loading the second rental van. I quickened my pace, handing Jamie my napkin filled with croissants. "Can you hold these for a sec?"

"Sure."

"Thanks. Hey, Hailey!" I said, grabbing the handle of Oscar's suitcase with my free hand. "Mi Jin promised to let us borrow two comics each for the flight. Want to come pick them out with me?"

Hailey's face lit up. "Okay!" She took off like a shot through the doors, and I followed, silently willing Jamie to come with me. "See you guys outside!"

Jamie pushed through the doors and held them open. I glanced over my shoulder and saw Oscar watching me, eyes slightly narrowed. I gave him my best attempt at a supportive-but-not-pushy smile, and then the doors swung shut.

After tossing Oscar's and my suitcases into the pile of bags Roland was still loading into the second van, I joined Hailey in the backseat. Jamie squeezed in next to me, and we started rifling through Mi Jin's for-comics-only backpack. She hopped on the van a minute later, snatching the bag out of Hailey's lap.

"I took the liberty of carefully curating a few personal recommendations," she informed us, carefully pulling out eight issues. "These two are Oscar's . . . Hailey, these are yours . . . Jamie . . . and Kat." Mi Jin handed me two *Guardians of the Galaxy* comics with a gracious smile. "Moondragon. You're welcome."

"Thanks," I said eagerly. Roland was climbing into the van in front of us, followed by Jess. Dad waved at me before getting in behind her. I glanced over my shoulder and saw Lidia shaking hands with Professor Guzmán. She called, "Let's go, Oscar!" before hopping into the front seat of our van next to the driver.

Oscar hurried out of the lobby, and I quickly turned my attention back to my comic. I sneaked a peek at him when he sat next to Mi Jin and pulled the van door closed, but his expression was impossible to read.

For most of the ride to the airport, Mi Jin told us about the next few episodes they were planning—a haunted bridge in China and an abandoned asylum in South Korea—but I barely listened. I was thinking about Jamie's explanation of psychic photography and how Sam had told Roland "not believing is just as powerful as believing." I believed in the Thing, and she appeared in my camera. She got out, and now she was real. She'd even left a comment on my last blog post. *I GOT OUT.*

But if I stopped believing in her . . .

I squeezed my eyes closed, fighting the urge to laugh.

Maybe I really was losing my mind. *Stop believing in the Thing, and she won't exist! Tinker Bell is dying, so clap if you believe in fairies!* But crazy or not, I'd have to figure out some way to get rid of the Thing once and for all.

I'd just started to doze off when we pulled up to the airport. Groggily, I followed everyone through all the baggage check-in lines, security lines, and customs lines. I thought I was doing a pretty good job hiding my exhaustion, but when we finally got to our gate, Dad pulled me aside.

"What's going on, Kat?"

"What?" I dropped my backpack onto one of the hard plastic chairs. "Nothing! Why?"

"Roland told me you were crying about something last night," Dad said, eyes filled with concern. "But you wouldn't say what. Is everything okay?"

"Oh, that. Um . . ." I couldn't tell anyone about the Thing, obviously. That would require explaining that I'd spent my whole life imagining this ridiculous other version of myself. And then I heard myself say:

"I got an invitation to Mom's bridal shower."

"Ah." Dad nodded sympathetically. "Kat, whether or not you go is totally up to—"

"I want to go."

The words spilled out before I'd fully grasped the thought. But once I said it, I knew it was the right thing to do. Not because I wanted to go—I didn't. Not because my mom wanted me to go—she'd be fine without me, just like always.

The Thing was my mother's ideal version of me. If I wanted it to stop haunting me, then I couldn't keep running away from either of them.

"It's March first," I told Dad. "I know it depends on the show's schedule, but I'll have to go back to Chelsea at some point. Mom said I need to get fitted for my bridesmaid dress."

Dad was smiling in a mostly proud, kind of sad way that made my chest ache a little. "We'll work it out with the schedule," he assured me. "If you want to be there, I'll make sure it happens."

"Thanks, Dad."

One of the flight attendants called for first-class passengers, and I waved at Jamie and Hailey as they followed their father to the line. I mulled over my plan as I waited to board. The thought of being in my mom's wedding still made me queasy. But if I could get through it, maybe the Thing—real or imaginary—would finally disappear.

After Roland helped me shove my backpack into the overhead bin, I sat down next to Oscar with a heavy sigh.

"You okay?" he asked.

"Yeah." I glanced at him. "You?"

"Fine." He went back to staring at the open comic in his lap, and I pulled out my phone. "Any more comments?"

"No," I said, lowering my voice, since Roland and Sam were sitting behind us. "Not since Maytrix kicked him off the forums. Hopefully he just gave up."

"Cool."

I didn't mention the other, anonymous comment.

After clicking *Will Attend* on the shower invitation from Grandma, I turned my phone off and half listened to the flight attendant go over safety stuff while Oscar read his comic. Ten minutes later, our plane was in the air, and he still hadn't turned the page.

"Okay, I have to ask," I said quietly. "Did you talk to Thiago about . . . you know . . ."

Oscar didn't look up. "Kind of."

I sat up straighter. "Kind of?"

"He sort of, um . . . brought it up first."

"I *knew* it!" I exclaimed, and Oscar pressed his lips together like he was trying not to smile. "I *so* knew it. What did he say? Did he tell you he likes you?"

"Not exactly. Um . . ." I watched as his face grew steadily redder. Then it hit me, and I gasped.

"Did he kiss you?" I shout-whispered.

Oscar's eyes widened. *"Shh!"*

"But did he?"

"Stop yelling!"

"I'm not yelling! Did he?"

"Yes, okay? Be quiet!"

"I am being quiet!"

"You're really not," Roland said mildly from the seat behind us. Oscar and I looked at each other for a second, then dissolved into silent, hysterical laughter. It was several minutes before I'd collected myself enough to speak again.

"That is *awesome*." I started to say more, then hesitated. In seventh grade, Trish had kissed this guy, Damien, at the winter dance, and she'd told me all about it. Every day. For weeks. In a *lot* of detail. I'd listened to it all, because I wanted to be a good friend. But Trish was a lot more into sharing that kind of stuff than I was.

Oscar was more like me, though. He kept most feelings to himself. On the other hand, he didn't have friends back home to e-mail like I did. And everyone deserved at least the option of having someone to get all share-y with.

"Do you want to talk about it?" I asked finally. He gave me a look, like he was considering it.

"Not yet. Maybe later?"

"Okay."

Oscar gave me a quick smile, and I smiled back. It dawned on me that despite the fact that we bickered almost constantly, Oscar really did trust me. And I really trusted him, too. After a minute of mental debate, I came to a decision.

"I have another theory about that girl," I said softly. "The ghost."

He looked up. "Really? What is it?"

"It's . . ." I paused to stifle a yawn. "Really, really complicated, and I didn't sleep at all last night. If I try to explain it right now, you'll think I'm crazy. Actually, you'll probably think I'm crazy no matter what."

"I mean, I already do a little bit," Oscar said dryly, and I tried to smile.

"Ha-ha. Either way, when we get to New York, can I tell you about it?"

"Of course."

"Thanks."

While I dug a tiny pillow and blanket out of my seat compartment and bunched them up behind my head, Oscar went back to pretending to read his comic. Within a few minutes, I fell asleep, and I didn't dream at all.

Edie Mills (born November 22, 1956) is an American actress known for her leading roles in many notable horror movies. She made her debut in 1972 in the low-budget *Mutant Cheerleaders Attack,* and while reviews of the film itself were almost universally negative, Mills's performance was widely praised. She was quickly cast in *The Monster in Her Closet,* which is considered to be her breakout film, solidifying her place among horror's greatest Scream Queens. Mills was named Best Actress at the Dark Cheese B-Movie Awards in 1979 for her performance as Debra St. James in *Den of the Undead.*

FILMOGRAPHY

MUTANT CHEERLEADERS ATTACK
JUNE 1972

When Kimmy Kickwell makes the cheerleading squad, she thinks high school's going to be nothing but football games and fun. But this squad's idea of fun isn't so much about *cheer* as it is *fear*, and their pep is contagious . . .

THE MONSTER IN HER CLOSET
FEBRUARY 1973

Carrie Butler forgot about her imaginary friend, Edgar, when she started middle school. But he never forgot her. And for her sweet sixteen, he's got one hell of a surprise party planned.

VAMPIRES OF NEW JERSEY
MAY 1974

Everyone in Hammerhead Bay is buzzing about the big surf competition . . . until the mysterious Maribel Mauls comes to town and starts making waves of her own. This summer, the shore is really going to suck.

CANNIBAL CLOWN CIRCUS
JULY 1975

Elephants! Acrobats! . . . Zombies? Trapeze artist Tina Soares loves the thrill of flight . . . but she'll need more than a safety net when this particular circus comes to town.

RETURN TO THE ASYLUM
JUNE 1976

Jackie Urns left her job at Queenswood Asylum after a traumatic incident rendered her mute. One year later, she's ready to return and face her demons.

THE DAME

MARCH 1977

Stella Shade is the city's top PI—a secret known to only a few police officials. When Stella moonlights as a waitress at an underground speakeasy to investigate rumors of a murderous spirit, all hell breaks loose. (Set in the 1920s, this film has the distinction of being Edie Mills's only historical work. It's also infamous for its highly unpopular twist ending, in which Edie's character is revealed to be the killer.)

THE COVEN'S CURSE

OCTOBER 1977

When Caroline Hahn returns home for a high-school reunion, she finds out her girlfriends have kept their old secret coven going. Only their rituals have gotten more intense. And this time, they aren't going to let Caroline break the pact . . .

A THOUSAND FANGS

JUNE 1978

Psychologist Brenda Doyle has the same nightmare every night— an enormous gaping mouth with a thousand fangs, swallowing her whole. But a dream is just a dream . . . until corpses with giant teeth marks start turning up all over town.

DEN OF THE UNDEAD

FEBRUARY 1979

When a group of archaeologists go missing during a dig, Debra St. James and her search-and-rescue team are dispatched. But when they find the not-quite-alive scientists, Debra starts to think this mission must fail for the sake of all mankind.

HOLLOW BOOKS

SEPTEMBER 1979

Amelia Hooper just wants a quiet life, and her new job at the quaint Brockensville Public Library gives her a chance at just that. But when Amelia discovers a locked room stocked with strange books—each filled with blank pages—her life becomes decidedly noisy.

INFECTION

MAY 1980

It shares all the symptoms of the common cold—until the third day, when the real infection reveals itself. Dr. Sandra Vix is used to treating patients with fevers and stuffy noses, but can she find a prescription for pure evil?

THE ASYLUM

MARCH 1981

In this controversial prequel to the beloved *Return to the Asylum,* Edie Mills plays the role of the Warden, the first movie's villain who terrorizes and ultimately kills Jackie Urns (also portrayed by Mills). Reception of the Warden's origin story was mixed, and *The Asylum*'s release launched a popular theory that Jackie Urns never existed and the events in *Return* happened entirely in the Warden's head.

CAMP HALF HELL

MAY 1982

The weapon: a curling iron. The victims: all counselors, picked off one by one. But Mel Sommers has seen enough horror movies to know that running does no good. She needs to face this killer once and for all. Only one will remain by the time the sun rises . . .

BEES?!

In this campy reimagining of Alfred Hitchcock's *The Birds*, schoolteacher Ann Hays fears the worst when her ex-fiancé's body is found covered in sting welts. The bees are coming . . .

WHAT SHE SEES IN THE MIRRORS

Largely criticized as being too cerebral, this film focuses on a woman with an unusual and disturbing phobia. Addilyn Cane cannot look people in the face; she can only look at their reflections. But no one realizes what she sees until it's too late.

MY GIRLFRIEND IS FROM PLUTO

It started as a joke. But now Nancy Riley's paranoid boyfriend actually thinks she's an alien—and he's managed to convince a group of conspiracy theorists that she's come to Earth to feed on human hearts.

INVASION OF THE FLESH–EATING RODENTS

When a new rabies vaccine goes horrifically wrong, veterinarian Katya Payne locks herself in her clinic, vowing not to leave until she finds a cure. But not if her furry former patients find her first . . .